Jacques' Escape

Library and Archives Canada Cataloguing in Publication

Kelly, Anne C., 1959–
    Jacques' escape / Anne C. Kelly

ISBN 978-1-7753717-1-7 (softcover)
Canadiana
LCC PS8621.E44115 J33 2019 | DDC JC813/.6—DC23
20190072628

This is a work of fiction. All names, characters, places, and events, with the exception of some well-known historical figures, are products of the author's imagination or used in a fictitious manner. Where real-life historical figures appear, incidents and dialogue concerning those persons are entirely fictional and are not intended to depict actual events or to change the fictional nature of the work.

Cover and illustrations by Helah Cooper
Book design by Jayme Spinks
Author photo by Ursula Handleigh

Printed and bound in Canada

100% TCF BIO GAS° PERMANENT

This book was set in Adobe Caslon, a typeface designed by Carol Twombly, and based on English typefounder William Caslon's printed specimen pages from 1734–1770.

Trap Door Books in an imprint of Nevermore Press, Ltd.

Nevermore Press, Ltd.
P.O. Box 369
Lunenburg, NS B0J 2C0
Canada

For my family,
with gratitude and love

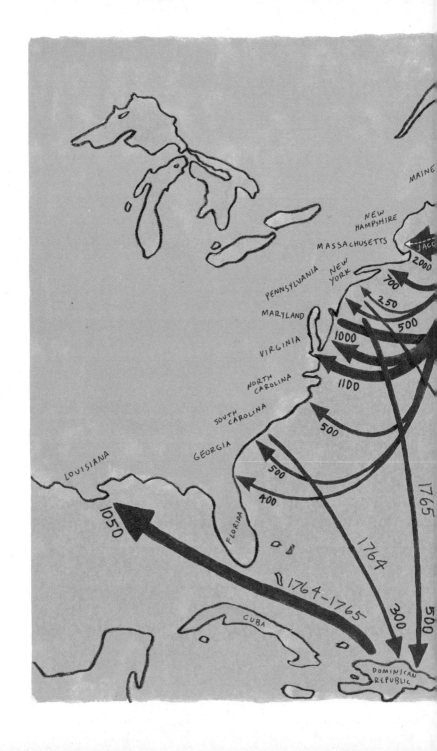

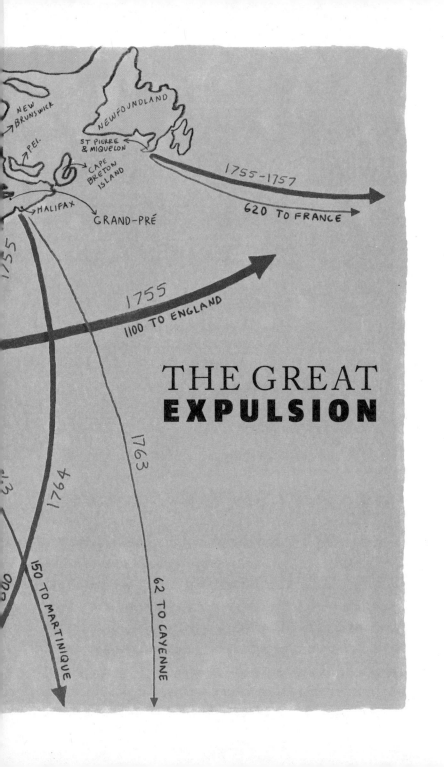

NEW BRUNSWICK

NEWFOUNDLAND

ST PIERRE & MIQUELON

P.E.I.

CAPE BRETON ISLAND

HALIFAX

GRAND-PRÉ

1755-1757

620 TO FRANCE

1755

1755

1100 TO ENGLAND

1763

1764

150 TO MARTINIQUE

62 TO CAYENNE

THE GREAT
EXPULSION

ONE
Papa's Story

"Étienne?" Jacques Terriot sat bolt upright in bed and stared around the pitch-black loft he shared with his brothers. Straining his ears, he could just make out the soft padding of Étienne's moccasins as he crept down the ladder. Michel stirred beside him, and Jacques slid back under the covers. He twisted his hands in the rough woollen blanket, forcing himself to lie still. It took all his strength not to fly after his brother and beg him not to go.

The outside door clicked shut.

Jacques buried his head in the straw mattress. At fourteen he was too old to cry, but he couldn't help the tears that ran down his cheeks. He bit his bottom lip to keep from sobbing out loud. Étienne has to go, he thought fiercely. He can't stay here with Papa any longer, not after last night.

Jacques shifted restlessly, seeing again Étienne's face, flushed with anger, as he argued with Papa.

"You're a coward, Papa," Étienne said, pushing his chair back from the supper table. "You sit here and do nothing! The English build their forts and make their laws and you do nothing!" He pounded his fist on the table. "We've been English prisoners for forty-two years! Forty-two years, Papa, since the maudit 1713 Treaty of Utrecht stole our lands and still you do nothing!"

Papa took a deep breath. "That's not true," he said gently. "We made an agreement with the English."

"Agreement?" Étienne spat the word. "You made a coward's deal!"

"We bargained for our freedom." Papa's voice hardened. "The English agreed that we could keep our language and our religion. They accepted our neutrality. Do you call that a coward's deal?"

"Yes!" Étienne's dark eyes flashed. "Because we're still English subjects! We should fight!"

Papa pushed back his chair and stood up. He glared at his son. "I won't have talk of war in this house!" he said.

"But Papa!" Étienne leapt to his feet, towering over his father. His cheeks were bright red. "We have to join the French! We have to fight for our land!"

"No."

"Because you're afraid?" Étienne taunted.

"Because I've seen fighting before." Papa sank back into his chair. "It's not exciting. It's horrible." He covered his eyes.

"But it'd be worth it! We'd be free!"

Papa looked up at him. "Do you think you'd be freer with a French governor than an English one?" he asked.

Étienne curled his lip. "Of course."

"Why?"

"Because we're French!"

"Non, Étienne." Papa picked up his clay pipe and pressed tobacco into the bowl. "We're not French. We're Acadian."

"What's the difference?" Étienne grasped the edge of the table as if he wanted to crush it in his big hands. He struggled to keep his voice low. "Your great-grandfather came from France!"

"Yes, he did," Papa agreed. "He came here because he was a farmer and he wanted to farm. He worked hard, building the dykes, stealing this land from the sea…"

"And then the English stole it from us!" Étienne yelled.

Papa looked up from his pipe. He struggled to keep his voice steady. "And did the French in Louisbourg help us then? Did the soldiers in Québec protect us?" He shook his head. "No! They didn't care then, and they don't care now! We're nothing to them."

Étienne let go of the table and shoved back against the wooden bench, almost knocking Michel to the floor. "You're a fool," he shouted. "A fool and a coward! But I'm not!" He clenched his fists. "I'm not going to put up with it any longer! I'm going to fight!"

Papa's hands shook as he laid down his pipe. "Étienne," he pleaded. "I know how you feel. I understand…"

"You understand nothing!" Étienne stormed from the room.

Now Étienne was leaving, and Jacques couldn't lie still any longer. He climbed out of bed and pulled on his heavy trousers, moccasins and deerskin jacket. He stuffed his long brown hair under his hat, tiptoed down the ladder and slipped outside into the early spring morning.

A thick fog blanketed the fields. Jacques strained to hear Étienne's horse as it galloped towards Grand-Pré, but all he could hear was the dull crash of the waves as they beat against the shore of the Minas Basin.

Jacques placed a log on the chopping block. He picked up the axe and swung it with all his strength. Splinters flew everywhere. He tossed the kindling into a pile and reached for another log. The steady rhythm of the chopping calmed him and soon a pile of wood towered beside him.

"Are you chopping wood for the whole village?" Papa asked from behind him. Jacques stiffened, but did not turn to face his father. "Étienne is gone," he said dully.

"I know."

"Why did you let him go?"

"I couldn't stop him."

Jacques threw the axe on the ground and spun around. His brown eyes blazed. "You could've tried!" he yelled. "You didn't even try."

"I couldn't stop him, Jacques." Papa laid his hand on his son's shoulder. "Étienne wants to fight…"

Jacques pulled away from his father's grasp. "So? What's wrong with that?"

"You too?" Papa asked. "Do you think I am a fool and a coward too?"

Jacques didn't answer. Papa sighed. "Jacques," he said softly. "I know it's hard for young men to understand, but sometimes you have to make compromises." He picked up the axe and leaned it against the stack of wood. "We can't beat the English by fighting—God knows we've tried. There's only one way we can win, by fighting with our ploughs and our families. Not with guns."

Jacques snorted.

"And we have won!" Papa continued. "This is our land. Even the English accept that."

"They're still our masters!"

"But they don't interfere. We still speak our language. They call us papists, oui, c'est vrai. But we can still go to Mass and baptize our babies…"

"As long as we behave!"

Papa face flushed. "Who cares?" he shouted. "They leave us alone. Do you really think war is the answer? Do you have any idea what that means?"

"It means freedom from the English!"

Papa lowered his voice with an effort. "It means people dying," he said. "Men, women, and children. It means cows and sheep and pigs killed. Crops destroyed. For what? So we don't have to swear allegiance to England?"

"Yes!"

"I'd rather swear the oath."

Then you are a coward, Jacques thought. He didn't say it out loud, but his father must have guessed because he nodded. "Ah, Jacques," he said. "You think I don't understand, but I do." He hesitated. "Grab a log and sit down," he said, waving toward the wood pile. "I want to tell you a story."

Jacques pulled out a large stump and sat down. The morning sun had burned away most of the fog, and he could see his father's face clearly as Papa crouched beside him.

"I know what war is really like," Papa said. "You know I took part in the attack on Colonel Noble eight years ago?"

Jacques nodded.

Papa stared at the ground. "I don't like to talk about it," he said. "So I never told you what happened. Maybe that was a mistake." He hesitated.

"I know the English were here, in Grand-Pré," Jacques said. "I remember seeing them in the market."

Papa nodded. "Most of the troops were from New England. Colonel Noble brought them here because of the attacks on Annapolis Royal. Small raiding parties of Mi'kmaq and French troops from Beaubassin kept trying to force the English out." Papa looked at Jacques and smiled sadly. "See, a lot of us felt then like you do now, so some of our young men joined in the raids."

"Did you?"

"Not at Annapolis Royal, no. Not until we got word of the French plan to send more reinforcements from Beaubassin. I thought with enough soldiers to support us, we could chase the English out of L'Acadie." Papa stood up and stretched. He grabbed a stump, dragged it closer to his son and sat down.

"We knew where the English were being billeted," Papa continued. "Our plan was to creep up on the houses. Most of us were young, hot-blooded Acadians, with a few French soldiers and Mi'kmaq men thrown in." Papa sighed. "It was February, the middle of winter. We pushed our way through the snow. It was dark and cold and..."

Jacques eyes glowed. "What happened?" he asked.

"Somehow we got there without being seen. God knows how. But we stopped outside one of the houses and waited for the rest of the French troops to arrive."

"And?"

"One of the Englishmen must have heard a noise." Papa stared off towards the meadow, but Jacques knew he wasn't seeing the long salt grass or the gulls soaring above the shore. "I don't know how he could hear anything. The wind was making an awful racket. But he must have. He opened the door. We all had to drop down and hide our faces in the snow."

"Did he see you?"

"Not that time. He closed the door and we moved in closer to the house. We got into position and waited." Papa glanced quickly at Jacques' face. "We were supposed to get French reinforcements, you see. But they didn't come. So we waited." Papa sighed. "Then the door opened again and this time we were spotted. The Englishman sounded the alarm! Soldiers started running all over the place."

"Did you shoot them?"

Papa stood up slowly, his eyes filling with tears. "Our leader was killed right away. Shot through the head. The noise was deafening; the muskets, the men crying and shouting…" After a long pause, he said, "I couldn't, I couldn't…"

Jacques jumped up, knocking the log over, and glared down at his father "You chickened out!"

Papa kept his eyes on the meadow. "The French soldiers came at last. They killed Colonel Noble and more than sixty of his troops. We drove them back to Annapolis Royal." Papa wiped the tears from his cheeks. "But it was all for nothing."

"What do you mean? The French won!"

"That battle, oui. But the next month, the English

were back." Papa studied Jacques' face. "So many people killed, and for what? It changed nothing in the end." He turned away and went back into the house.

Jacques' hands trembled, as he threw the stump back on the woodpile. His eyes stung as he blinked back tears. "He's a coward," he muttered, "just like Étienne said. Scared of the noise…" His chest ached. From inside the house he could hear his year-old sister, Marguerite, giggling at Maman's singing as she set the table. Smoke trickled out of the chimney along with the sweet smell of porridge.

Jacques turned and ran into the field like an escaping prisoner.

TWO

A Summoning

Jacques sat on a wooden stool beside the door, the last light of the September evening shining through the glass window. He studied the small wooden goose he was carving. His brother-in-law, Henri, sat beside the fireplace, talking to Papa. Maman and his sister Anne worked on the large, brightly-coloured quilt spread out over the table. Marguerite babbled to herself on the floor beside them.

"I tell you. I don't like it," Henri said.

Jacques looked up from his whittling in surprise. Henri's normally calm voice was angry.

"It's just a meeting, Henri." Papa said. He settled back in his chair and took his pipe out of his pocket. "There's nothing sinister in that."

"Non?" Henri leaned forward, his huge hands planted on his knees. "Then tell me why there's no word from our deputies in Halifax. They should be part of any meeting we have with the English." He dropped his voice to a whisper. "There's a rumour that Governor Lawrence threw them into jail for refusing to take the loyalty oath."

Papa sighed. "We took an oath already."

"One of neutrality," Henri said.

"True." Papa agreed. "Governor Philips agreed to our neutrality when the English first took over. So did Cornwallis after him. They knew we didn't want to fight. Governor Lawrence will accept that too, eventually."

"I don't know." Henri shifted in his chair. He glanced quickly at his wife and mother-in-law. "I don't like what I hear."

Jacques stared at Henri, his carving forgotten. Though gentle in nature, Henri was a large man and owned a blacksmith shop in the village. People from all around Minas came to him to have their horses shod and to buy nails and iron tools. Unlike most of the Acadians, Henri could speak some English, so even the soldiers from Fort Edward and from Colonel Winslow's encampment in Grand-Pré came to him for supplies or gossip. Henri was often the first to get news, and his opinions were accepted almost without question, so Jacques listened closely.

"Lawrence doesn't like us," Henri continued. "He never did. And after the surrender at Beauséjour, he feels he's right not to trust us. Think about it! The French surrender and four hundred Acadians, neutral Acadians, are found inside the fort!"

"But they had to fight!" Jacques blurted out. "Everyone knows that! The French commander threatened them. He said he'd kill them if they didn't fight! Even Governor Lawrence has to understand that!"

Henri looked at him. "Lawrence understands that his worst fear came true. Acadians helping the French to fight."

"Well, we should be," Jacques muttered. "We should be fighting with the French, not worrying about swearing the oath of allegiance to an English king!"

"Enough, Jacques," Papa said. He glanced at Maman and Anne talking quietly, at the baby crawling on the floor.

"But if we joined the French…"

"We could share their glorious victories?" Henri mocked. "Beauséjour was a real victory, wasn't it?" He shook his head. "The fort was taken just two days after it was attacked, and the Acadians caught there gave Lawrence the excuse he wanted. Now he'll make us pay." Henri hesitated. "You know François Landry? He has relatives in the area around Chignecto." Henri looked closely at Papa. "He heard that Étienne was there."

"At Beauséjour?" Papa dropped his head into his hands, as if it was suddenly too heavy to hold up. "Ah, mon Dieu!"

"Maybe it isn't true." Henri shrugged. "Who knows what is true these days?"

"I bet he was!" Jacques said, his eyes bright. "I bet he was there, right in the middle of the fighting. Firing his musket at the redcoats!"

"Jacques!" Papa cried. "This isn't a game!" He gripped the empty pipe in his hands. "If he was there, then where is he now? In an English prison in Halifax?" His eyes filled with tears. "Or worse?"

"Now Papa," Henri said softly. "We don't even know if he was there." He glanced again at the women.

Papa nodded. He wiped his eyes on his sleeve. His hands shook as he took his tobacco pouch from his pocket and filled his pipe. He lit it and puffed in silence.

Jacques sulked, twisting his carving in his hands. Papa's words stung. He knew what had happened at Beauséjour wasn't a game—he wasn't a child! But he was sure that Étienne had been there, and that his brother had welcomed the chance to fight, no matter what happened afterwards.

"The soldiers are really settling down here at Grand-Pré." Henri's voice jerked Jacques back to the present. "Their commander, Colonel Winslow, has taken over the priest's house and the church. His men are building pickets all around the area, making it into a camp. They're even cutting down any willows beside the fence."

"He's a cautious man." Papa blew smoke towards the ceiling. "Maybe that's what this meeting is all about, to explain what he wants from us."

"Or to demand more food," Henri said. "He's already commandeering meat, vegetables and flour without payment." He stood up and stretched, his hands almost brushing the rafters. "I still don't like it. Every man and boy ordered to attend a meeting. Something's going on, I'm sure of it."

"Oh, Henri," Anne said. She walked over and laid her hand on her husband's arm. "You worry too much."

Henri smiled. "Maybe I do. But I have a wife to protect and soon a child too." Anne blushed and rubbed her stomach, where her baby was just beginning to show.

"And a fine father you'll be," she teased, "gloomy all the time."

"Jamais!" Henri's face burst into a grin. "I'll show you what kind of papa I'll be." He grabbed Marguerite from the floor beside the fire and spun her around. The little girl shrieked with laughter. Henri danced around the room. Papa grinned at Maman, and Anne collapsed giggling into a straight-backed chair.

A smile tugged at Jacques' lips. Henri placed Marguerite on the floor, and she crawled over to Jacques and pulled herself up against his knee. He ruffled her hair, then held out the little wooden goose he was carving. Marguerite grabbed the toy and plopped down, cooing happily. Jacques slipped outside.

The evening air was cool. Jacques surveyed the yard with a strange lump in his throat. In the kitchen garden next to the house, green leaves from the carrots and turnips poked through the wilting herbs and shrivelled bean plants. Soon it would be time to rake the dark, rich soil in preparation for winter. Jacques wandered past the chicken coop and the barn to the edge of the fields. As far as he could see, the wheat grew tall and golden, waiting to be cut and stacked. Jacques closed his eyes and took a deep breath, inhaling the sweet, dusty scent of ripe grain.

Suddenly, he heard hooves thundering up the path behind him. He spun around. "Mon Dieu!" he shouted. "You scared me!"

His brother Michel grinned as he slid off the stocky brown horse his family used for riding and pulling their cart. His face was wind-burnt, and his light brown hair stuck up in all directions. "Wow!" he said. "You should've seen us go!" He stroked the horse's neck. "We left the others in the dust, didn't we, boy?"

Jacques grinned back at his brother. "Bravo!"

"We were racing against Daniel and Simon, over in

the west field. Old Pierre here was galloping full-out." Michel's brown eyes shone. "We almost ran right over the dyke!"

"Good thing you stopped!"

"Yeah!" Michel rubbed the horse's nose affectionately. "Then we almost ran into an English patrol."

Jacques' grin faded. "Where?"

"By the church. Redcoats."

"Red? Not Winslow's men then." Unlike the English regiments, Jacques knew the New England provincial troops that had come to Grand-Pré with Winslow wore blue tunics.

"Non. I think they were coming back from Pisiquid. Daniel and Simon kept going up the road, but Pierre and me cut across the field." Michel stroked Pierre's nose again. "We didn't want anything to do with them, did we boy?" He led the horse into the barn.

Jacques followed him into the warm darkness. "Was it a big patrol?" he asked.

Michel shrugged. "Three or four men, I think. I didn't get too close." He rubbed the horse gently with an old wool blanket. "Why?"

"Colonel Winslow's issued a proclamation. He wants…" Jacques' voice hardened. "He demands that all the men in Minas meet him in the church tomorrow."

"What for?"

"Nobody knows." Jacques piled some hay in Pierre's stall and turned to go. "But Henri is worried."

Michel patted the horse again and followed his brother out of the barn. "Do I have to go too?"

Jacques studied him. Michel was almost twelve, but

small and slight, almost girlish. His bottom lip trembled. Jacques scowled. "Yes," he said harshly. "Winslow wants all boys ten years and older. Even crybaby boys."

"But I don't want to!"

"We don't have a choice." Jacques spat into the dirt. "We have to do what Winslow tells us!"

"But Governor Lawrence knows we don't want to fight." Michel's voice shook. "That's what Papa said. So what's Winslow going to do?"

"Who knows?" Jacques forced a smile, and punched Michel softly on the arm. "But don't worry. I mean, what can he do?"

THREE
Betrayal

Jacques stared at Colonel John Winslow in alarm. Surely, he didn't mean...he couldn't mean what he said. The words echoed dully in Jacques' head: "Your lands...cattle...livestock...forfeited to the Crown...and you yourselves...removed from...His Majesty's Province."

Removed. Sent away. Deported.

Jacques shoved his hands into the pockets of his thick wool trousers to hide their shaking. Henri was right; Lawrence did want to get rid of them. The English had threatened to deport them before, but no one had taken the threats seriously.

Colonel Winslow of the English Provincial Troops was deadly serious. Jacques studied the officer. He stood tall and straight as a soldier should, but he moved his shoulders inside his blue and red officer's tunic as if it didn't fit comfortably. Henri stood beside him, staring in disbelief as he struggled to translate the officer's words. Winslow kept his eyes focused on the words of the proclamation.

Jacques tried to shift his weight on the hard, wooden

bench. He was squeezed so tightly between Papa and Michel he could barely breathe. Men overflowed the benches and leaned against the barrels of rice and flour stored in the church for the soldiers.

Colonel Winslow lowered the proclamation and started walking down the aisle. For a second, no one else moved. Then a young boy behind Jacques began to sob and a man's voice yelled, "You can't do this!"

Jacques recognized the speaker, Josef Babin, a farmer from the other side of Grand-Pré. Jacques had been to his farm once for a wedding. After the ceremony, there had been a lavish feast, with fiddles and dancing. The next morning, the men and boys had joined together to build a house for the young couple. A house that the English were now stealing.

Winslow stopped and looked at Josef. His eyes softened and he opened his mouth to speak. He looked almost sorry, Jacques thought, wondering what the English officer would say. But Winslow just shook his head and turned away, passing through the door without comment.

Chaos erupted as other angry voices joined Josef's. Jacques and Papa were shoved aside as their neighbours rushed to the doors, yelling and cursing. They were turned back by the guards, and the doors were closed and locked.

Jacques grabbed Papa's arm. "Can they really do this?" he cried. "Can they really send us away?"

Papa shook his head, stunned. "I don't know," he said. "I just don't know."

"But they can't send us all away," interrupted Michel,

tears filling his eyes. "They just can't. There are too many of us."

"That's right," Jacques agreed, struggling to stay calm. "There are close to four hundred men here in Grand-Pré. Plus the women and children. Then there's Port Royal and Chignecto…They wouldn't have enough ships."

"I don't know," Papa said again. "We'll have to wait and see." He pushed his way through the crowd towards Henri.

Jacques looked after him in disbelief. "I'm not going to wait!" he said.

"What do you mean?" asked Michel. "What else can we do?"

"Fight."

"But how?" Michel glanced at the soldiers by the door. "We have no weapons, and the English…"

"Not here," Jacques whispered. "I have to get away. I have to find Étienne."

"But we're prisoners here."

"Then I'll have to find a way to escape."

"But Papa…"

"Papa doesn't understand." Jacques grabbed his younger brother by the collar. "And if you tell…"

"I won't," Michel answered. "But what if you get caught?"

Jacques dropped his arms. "Don't worry. I'm not going to get caught, but first I have to find a way out."

For a week Jacques watched and waited. At night the men and boys were kept in the church under the watchful eyes of the blue-coated soldiers. Work parties were sent out every morning to harvest the grain still standing in the fields. Jacques joined the others, sweating in the September sun, swinging his scythe, hour after hour.

19

The wheat was then sent to the mill to be ground. Anger surged through him as he watched cartloads of flour going not into Acadian homes but into the kitchens of the English troops. He said nothing.

Around the camp, the newly-erected fence towered over Jacques, its logs so close together that even a mouse couldn't squeeze through. As Henri had predicted, Colonel Winslow was taking no chances. Hundreds of small fires burned throughout the camp, where wives and children met to have supper with their men before going home to empty houses.

"Jacques, you're not eating," Maman said one evening. "Do you feel all right?"

"Just tired." Jacques tried to smile. Maman and Marguerite weren't imprisoned with the men but were allowed to visit freely and bring them meals. "We cut the east field today. The soldiers want to finish harvesting before it rains." He stretched. "I think I'll lie down for a while." He kissed his mother's cheek. "See you tomorrow."

He slipped away from the campfire where his family was sitting. But Jacques didn't head to the church where his bedroll was waiting. For the hundredth time he began to pace along the walls of the encampment. After a week, he was no closer to escaping, and the anger and frustration made him feel as tight as a bowstring. He turned sharply at a sound behind him.

"It's only me." Michel fell into step with his brother and they walked on in silence. "It won't be easy, will it?" Michel asked at last.

"Non, but I'll find a way."

"Henri said he overheard some of the English soldiers

talking at the forge," Michel said. "The soldiers are saying Winslow doesn't agree with what's happening." Michel stopped and grabbed Jacques by the arm. "Maybe," his voice was excited. "Maybe he'll let us stay!"

"Non. Winslow is a soldier. He'll follow orders." Jacques pulled away from his brother's grip. "I just need to find a way to get out of the camp. And I will do it. Just wait and see!"

"How? The soldiers patrol all the time, even at night. There's roll call and sentries and…"

"I know," he said harshly. "But I won't give up!" He shoved his hands in his pockets and stalked away.

The next morning was wet and windy. The men hid inside the church, playing tric-trac and muttering about the weather. Jacques lay on his blanket, his mind full of wild ideas. He saw himself punching a sentry and stealing his musket. He saw himself climbing the wall like a thief in the night. Wild ideas, but no plan that would work.

Suddenly the door of the church flew open and a sentry burst into the room. His blue tunic was dripping wet, and water ran off his hat in rivulets. His mouth was twisted and angry.

"Get your coats," he barked. "One of the dykes has started to collapse. The hole has to be repaired before the tide comes in."

No one moved. The soldier swore. "Everyone," he screamed. "Now!" The door slammed behind him.

Jacques grabbed his jacket. Around him men cursed as they pulled on woollen hats and heavy leather boots. Jacques' heart pounded. Maybe…he thought. Just maybe this is my chance!

The men lined up outside, their heads down to keep off the rain. The sentry was joined by a sergeant and two other soldiers, who scowled at the prisoners as they handed out spades and pitchforks. No one bothered with roll call. Jacques grinned.

The sergeant bellowed an order and the ragged line marched out of the gate. The road was slippery with mud. The fields were hidden in a thick grey fog. Jacques' grin widened. It was perfect!

FOUR

Escape

They were drenched before they reached the end of the path leading to the shore. The fog hid the water but Jacques could hear the waves swishing like the wind rustling through the leaves of the trees. He could just make out the spot where the dyke had started to collapse, the grassy bank sliding down towards the beach. The rain was eating a channel into the mud, threatening to open the field to the rising tide. It wouldn't take a big hole, Jacques knew, to allow the sea to pour into the meadow and ruin the crops.

For two hours Jacques laboured under the indifferent eyes of the guards. Sweat mixed with rain ran down his face. He struggled along with the other men and boys to cut new bricks of sod from the marsh and lay them into the gap, fitting them together like a giant jigsaw puzzle.

Finally, the soldiers called a halt. Water ran down into Jacques' collar as he straightened up to catch his breath. He spotted Michel crouched against the bank, trying to stay dry. Papa and Henri were nowhere in sight. He made his way over to his brother. "At last," he said, squatting down beside his brother. "This is perfect!"

"Perfect?" Michel blinked back tears. "It's miserable! I'm soaking wet and I keep slipping…" His jacket and trousers were covered with mud.

"Exactly!" Jacques grinned. "Everyone is so miserable, they aren't paying attention." He pointed towards the guards, huddled together at one corner of the field. They were talking in low voices, gesturing towards the half-finished dyke.

Jacques' grin faded. "I have to go now," he said. "They might decide to go back to camp. This might be my only chance."

Michel's eyes filled with tears. "Do you have to go?"

Jacques stood up and pulled the younger boy up beside him. "You know I do," he said gently. "I can't live like this—a prisoner in my own home. I can't sit and wait to be sent away." He hugged Michel quickly. "Tell Papa…" His throat tightened. "Tell him…" He stopped and turned away.

"Tell Papa what?" Michel asked, but Jacques shook his head. He began to move slowly along the dyke, keeping his eyes on the soldiers. The small group broke apart; the sergeant waved his arm towards the Acadians and one of the guards barked an order. Jacques turned and ran.

And fell. Merde! he thought. Did they see me? He wiped the mud and rain from his face, straining to see through the drizzle. The guard was still yelling, but there was no alarm in his voice. Jacques crawled along the ground, the cold, watery clay seeping into his sleeves and through the buttons of his jacket. When he reached the corner of the field, he stood up slowly. Michel and the others were lost in the fog. Jacques grinned again. It would be so easy to defeat soldiers like these! He wiped the dirt from his mouth and eyes, climbed the mound that separated the fields, and began to wade towards the nearest farm.

In spite of the rain, he had no problem finding his way. Like most of the boys in Grand-Pré he had helped to plant and harvest these marshes ever since he could remember.

He was exhausted when he reached the orchard at the back of Monsieur Thibeau's farm, overlooking the Minas Basin. The apple trees were short and sturdy, with thick, gnarled limbs reaching down to the ground. Jacques pulled himself up into one of the trees and settled into the cleft between two branches. The leaves provided some protection from the downpour. He leaned his head against the rough bark and breathed in the sweet smell of apples.

It was dark before he stirred. The rain had stopped, and the moon peeped out from behind the clouds, throwing faint shadows on the ground. He slid down from his perch and stretched. His body ached with the cold, and his clothes and hair were stiff with mud. He splashed water from a puddle over his face and hands and wiped them on his shirt. His stomach growled. The apples on the tree were sour enough to twist his mouth, but he crunched one as he leaned against the tree and plotted his next move.

I need to find Étienne, he thought. But where is he? Hiding in the woods with the Mi'kmaq? In prison in Halifax? Or in Louisbourg with the French garrison there? Jacques threw the apple core into the woods and hugged himself to get warm. The truth was that he'd been so focused on escaping, on getting out of Winslow's camp, that he hadn't thought about where he would go next.

An owl hooted and he shivered. I can't just stay here, he thought. I'll keep walking up the coast until I get to Pisiquid and then head to Tatamagouche. From Tatamagouche he could try to catch a boat to the French fortress of Louisbourg. Or he could head south to the new English settlement at Halifax. That would be dangerous, but perhaps he could meet up with the deputies who had been sent from Grand-Pré to negotiate with the Governor. Maybe they would have news of the fighting or of his brother.

Jacques had been to Tatamagouche once before with his father. Papa, like many of his neighbours, used to drive his cattle there to ship them illegally to the French fortress. The trip took us a week last time, Jacques thought. The cows were so slow! He sighed. It probably won't be any quicker this time either. The soldiers will know at roll call tonight that I'm gone. I'll have to travel by night and keep my eyes open for English patrols.

He brushed some of the mud off his wool pants, stuffed some apples into his pockets, and started off.

The wind hit Jacques as soon as he stepped out of the

orchard. It was cold and damp with spray, and he pulled his jacket tighter. He kept his head down as he trudged along the top of the cliff. His leather boots squished with every step.

The path ended abruptly in a tangle of bushes. Jacques swore. The faint light of the moon nearly disappeared as he pushed into the trees. He stretched his arms out in front of him like a blind man. Branches whipped his face, and unseen roots sent him flying.

The night dragged on. Jacques struggled through patches of deep woods and fought the wind in the clearings at the top of the cliffs. By dawn he could barely put one foot in front of the other. Finally, he staggered through a break in the trees and fell.

He lay on the wet ground, too tired to move, listening to the crashing of the waves and the rustling of the wind in the leaves. The sky was turning pink, and a few crows called loudly to each other. Far above his head an eagle soared, but nothing else moved. He groaned, then forced himself to his knees to look around.

Directly in front of him was the large grassy wall of a dyke. Jacques crawled up and cautiously lifted his head. The meadow on the other side was partially cut, the long marsh grass lying in bundles along the far edge of the dyke. To his left he could see a farmhouse. Bien! he thought. Pisiquid! I made it! He strained his eyes, looking for movement or any signs of life, but the house and yard appeared deserted.

Jacques crawled back into the woods and stood up slowly. I'll have to try the farmhouse, he thought. I need something to eat! And maybe some dry clothes. But not now. There might be soldiers around. He climbed awkwardly into the crook of a tree not far from the edge of the field. It was hard and uncomfortable, but the sun was warm. Jacques' eyelids drooped. He leaned his head against the strong bough and fell asleep.

He woke with a start! Voices were shouting—English voices! Jacques jumped down from the tree, staggered and almost fell. His legs burned; he clung to a branch while the blood flowed back into his cramped muscles. The sun was shining. Jacques dropped flat on the ground and crawled towards the voices.

In the meadow, fifteen or twenty men were working, cutting the grass with their scythes and tying it into bundles. Soldiers wandered among the workers, the bright reds and blues of their coats vivid against the green of the field. From time to time they shouted orders at the Acadians. Jacques relaxed. It was just a work party— there was no urgency in the voices and no one came into the woods looking for a missing Acadian boy.

The ground was drier and Jacques stretched out, making sure he was well-hidden by the trees. He stared at the men, trying to see if any of them looked familiar. But they were too far away to see clearly, and Jacques' eyes were heavy. Soon he fell asleep again.

It was almost dark when he woke. There was no sign of the workers or the soldiers.

Jacques' stomach rumbled—it had been almost two days since he'd had more than apples to eat. He skirted the meadow and approached the farmhouse.

He stopped in the yard, studying the house and outbuildings. He had no idea if the men were being

held captive here, as in Grand-Pré, but candles were burning in the window, and smoke curled lazily out of the chimney. Jacques edged towards the house. He was almost at the door when it opened and a girl came out. She saw Jacques and jumped.

"Shhh…" Jacques put his finger to his lips. "I won't hurt you. I'm just looking for something to eat."

The girl shrank back to the door. "Who are you?" she asked.

"A friend who needs food."

"You're filthy!"

Jacques looked down at his mud-caked clothes. "I've been sleeping rough," he said.

"What are you doing here?"

"Please," he said softly. "The soldiers…"

The girl hesitated, and then beckoned Jacques inside. He closed the door behind him. Immediately she turned, blocking him from the rest of the room. She was small but sturdy, around his own age, with black hair and sky-blue eyes. She trembled, clearly frightened, but held her ground.

"Who are you and what are you doing here?" she repeated.

"My name is Jacques Terriot," he answered. He peered into the room. In the semi-darkness he could make out a stone fireplace with a kettle hanging over the fire and a sturdy wooden table. An older woman was sitting at the table, a patchwork quilt spread out in front of her. She stared at Jacques intently. He spoke to her. "I'm from Grand-Pré."

The woman got up and stood beside her daughter. "They told us all the men and boys were taken prisoner," she said. "How did you get away?"

"I escaped," Jacques said simply. "I'm going to Louisburg to join the French."

"Shh!" The woman looked around quickly. "We don't even whisper such things. The soldiers…"

"What can they do?" Jacques clenched his fists. "They have already taken our lands and our farms. They want to send us away. What else can we do but fight?"

"Leave my house." The woman turned her back and sat down again at the table. "I won't allow such violent talk here."

"Please," Jacques pleaded. "I just need something to eat."

"Go."

Jacques looked at the girl, still standing in the doorway. She refused to meet his eyes.

Sighing, he opened the door and eased back into the night.

He leaned against the side of the house. It was getting darker and he longed to be on his way. But his stomach was sharp with hunger. Should he try another house? Or did all the Acadians in Pisiquid feel the same? Cowards, he muttered.

The door of the house opened and the young girl slipped out. Silently she handed Jacques a packet wrapped in a rough cotton cloth.

Jacques smiled. "Merci," he said. The girl smiled shyly and went back into the house. Jacques unwrapped the cloth. Inside he found two slices of heavy homemade bread, some cheese, and an onion. He broke a piece off the bread and cheese and shoved it into his mouth. It tasted delicious! He sat down against the wall of the house and devoured his meal. When the last crumb was gone, he slipped back into the woods and started searching for the road that led to Tatamagouche.

The night passed uneventfully. A bright moon lit the way. After struggling through the woods for a couple of hours, he stumbled onto the road. He followed it as warily as a white-tailed deer, but he saw no one. As morning came, he found a hole in an old willow that had been hollowed out by some animal before him. It was cramped but warm, and with relief, he fell asleep.

Again, he woke suddenly. The bright September sun was just sinking behind the treetops. Jacques could hear horses as he peered out of his hiding place. There were five soldiers on the road, all wearing blue tunics. They had reined in their mounts and were clustered around their sergeant.

They spoke in English, but Jacques didn't need words to understand. He drew his head inside, terror running through him like a knife.

The horses crashed through the underbrush close by his tree. One stopped beside him and snorted. Jacques pressed himself deeper into the hole and held his breath.

The sunlight faded to grey and then to black as the soldiers hunted through the bushes. At last, the sergeant called to his men and they galloped off towards Pisiquid. Jacques let out his breath in a gasp. That was close, he thought, wiggling out of his hiding place. He looked around quickly and stood up.

Without warning, he was hit from behind.

FIVE

An Unexpected Meeting

As he struck the ground, his attacker clamped his hand over Jacques' mouth. Jacques turned and twisted, struggling to break free.

"Keep still."

Jacques stopped, surprised. The words were French; the voice familiar.

His attacker rolled off Jacques and lay beside him. Jacques turned his head. Two dark brown eyes smiled at him.

"Étienne?" he began, but his brother shook his head. He touched his finger to his lips.

The two boys lay without speaking. Jacques strained his ears until the last hoof beats faded into silence. Only then did Étienne move. "Mon Dieu!" he said. "That was a close one."

Jacques threw his arms around Étienne and squeezed. For a moment he said nothing. Then he pushed his brother away. "Where were you?" he babbled. "I didn't see you and the English soldiers..."

Étienne put his hand over Jacques' mouth. "Pas ici,"

he said. "There may be more. Come on." He crawled into the underbrush and disappeared. Jacques followed on his hands and knees. Just inside, the ground dipped, forming a small ditch completely hidden by the bushes. Jacques squirmed down the side and twisted around to lie beside Étienne. It was a tight fit. He could just make out the road through the leaves

"I've been walking for almost a week," Étienne said. "Trying to make my way back to Grand-Pré. But it was slow going, travelling at night I was afraid I wouldn't make it in time. So I took a chance and I decided to start a little earlier." He flashed a grin at Jacques. "Obviously not a good idea. I heard the horses and hid, but I guess they must have got a glimpse of me." His smile faded. "I was just thanking God for keeping me safe, when I saw you, popping out of that hole in the tree." He rolled on his side and studied the younger boy. "What are you doing here? Besides trying to get me caught by the English?"

"I was looking for you," said Jacques. "I want to come and fight with you!"

Étienne held up his hand. "Why? What happened?"

"The English," Jacques said bitterly. "They've rounded up all the men and boys. They're keeping them prisoners in the church. They've taken our farms, our cattle…" He gritted his teeth to keep from shouting. "They're going to deport us."

Étienne nodded grimly. "I just came from Tatamagouche. The English have already emptied the village completely."

"That's where I was going to go!"

Étienne stared towards the road, while his hands tore at the grass in front of him. "I was hoping I'd be in time to warn you. But it's too late." He hesitated. "How are Maman and Papa?" he asked softly.

Jacques crossed his arms and rested his chin on his hands. "Confused. Scared. Papa doesn't believe they'll send us away." He stared straight ahead. "He doesn't want to believe it."

"I wanted to warn Papa and the others," Étienne repeated. "To tell them to fight." He dug his nails into the earth.

"Did you fight, Étienne?" Jacques grabbed his brother's arm. "Were you at Beauséjour?"

Étienne glanced at his eager face, then looked away. "Yes, I was there."

"But you got away!"

"I was taken prisoner," he said with a shrug. "I escaped."

"What luck!"

"Yes," Étienne said, with a strange smile. "I was lucky." His face flushed. "We shouldn't have lost! But the other Acadians didn't have the heart to fight…"

"Cowards."

The two boys sat in silence.

"After I escaped," Étienne said finally, "I went to Halifax. I had to hide, of course, but still I heard rumours. That our deputies were in prison. That Lawrence planned to deport us all. So I rushed here, and was almost betrayed to the English by my own brother!"

"Were those soldiers from Halifax?"

"Non. Probably from Pisiquid, what they call Fort Edward."

"Why were they after you?"

Étienne didn't answer.

"Just because you escaped? Is Lawrence that determined to get every Acadian?"

"Non, mais…" He took a deep breath. "I killed a soldier while I was escaping. Knifed him." Étienne stared at his hands as if he could still see the blood.

Jacques' stomach churned. He stared at the ground as a cold chill ran down his back.

"It doesn't matter!" Étienne said harshly. "They're our enemies. I was glad to do it!"

Jacques looked closely at his brother. For the first time he noticed the dark circles under his eyes and the lines around his mouth. The defiance in his voice was shrill, as though Étienne was trying to convince himself as well. Jacques nodded.

"What'll you do now?"

"Go to Québec and join the forces there. Keep on fighting!" Étienne's head jerked up. "Listen!"

Jacques strained his ears. In the distance he could hear hoof beats. They were heading towards them!

"Stay here!" Étienne whispered. "I'll lead them away."

"But…" Jacques protested.

"Do it!" Étienne ordered. "They'll keep searching until they find me. And I don't want you…" He broke off and wiggled out of the underbrush. Before he straightened up, he whispered, "À bientôt, mon frère. Take care." Then he turned and ran.

A horse broke into the woods ahead of the others. Its rider dropped to the ground, yelling, "There he is!" Twigs snapped as he crashed into Étienne.

Jacques crawled out of the bushes and flung himself on top of the soldier. The man grunted in surprise.

Jacques tightened his arm around the man's neck and rolled him off his brother. "Run!" he gasped.

Étienne ran.

The sergeant and the other men rode into the clearing.

"Over there," said the first man, clawing free from Jacques' grip. His powerful hands held Jacques' wrists, forcing him onto his stomach. "Throw me some rope— I'll deal with this one."

Jacques cried out as the ropes bit into his flesh, then lay quietly, listening. Above the angry breathing of his captor, he could hear twigs cracking and the heavy tread of the soldiers' boots. He closed his eyes. Run, Étienne, he thought, willing his strength to his brother. Run!

After what seemed like hours, the soldiers returned to the clearing. Jacques lifted his head. There was no sign of Étienne.

"He's gone, but he won't get far in that wood." The sergeant wiped blood from a long scratch on his face and swore. "Dirty little French murderer. Wait till I get my hands on him." He glanced down at Jacques. "We set a trap to catch one traitor and snared a second one. Who are you?"

Jacques stared at the sergeant without speaking. His guard pulled him roughly to his feet. "Answer him," he ordered.

The sergeant bared his teeth. "Or perhaps you don't understand me? Parlez-vous English?"

The men laughed. Jacques said nothing.

"Well, you'll understand this!" The sergeant's large fist cracked against his face. Jacques fell. The soldiers laughed again.

Jacques struggled to his knees. Blood poured from his nose, staining his jacket. The rope bit into his wrists, and his hands were numb. Still he said nothing.

The sergeant shrugged. "Take him with us," he ordered. "Colonel Winslow can decide what to do with him."

The guard tied Jacques on the horse behind him. His head bumped against the man's back as they rode. His relief over Étienne's escape hardened into anger. His determination to fight against these English deepened as the horses galloped back towards Grand-Pré.

SIX

Detained

It was early morning when they arrived. Jacques was surprised to see a huge crowd outside the church. The noise was deafening. People were milling around, calling out to each other. Women were crying, huddled together in groups, ignoring the children screaming and running all over. Soldiers were shouting orders and forcing some of the young men into a ragged line. Jacques scanned the crowd for Papa and Michel, but he couldn't see them anywhere. The sergeant pulled him roughly from the horse, and he stumbled and fell at the edge of the crowd.

Suddenly he saw his mother, running towards him. She threw her arms around him. "Oh thank God," she cried. "You're here! We were so worried."

Jacques pulled away and stood up. "What's going on?" he asked.

"Winslow is putting some of the young men onto the ships now," she said. "The ships aren't ready to go yet, but a lot of the boys feel like you do, and Winslow doesn't want a rebellion."

Jacques studied the crowd again. "It doesn't look very organized."

"Most of the soldiers don't speak French, but they expect everyone to understand," she said. "I can, a little, but..."

Jacques looked at her with surprise. "Tu parles anglais?"

Maman put her finger to her lips and whispered. "Un peu. I used to help my father when he traded with the merchants from New England." She glanced at the soldiers. "I don't want them to know. This way I can try to help."

Jacques stared at her for a moment, then nodded. "Where is Michel?" he asked. "And Papa?"

"Still in the Church."

Jacques leaned closer to his mother. "I saw Étienne," he said softly.

Her face lit up with joy. "Where? Is he here? Is he okay?"

"Non, Maman," he said bitterly. "He's not okay. He was running away from the English when I saw him. That's how they caught me. But at least he's fighting!"

"Oh, Jacques." Maman pulled him close and rested her cheek on his hair. "Do you still believe it is better to fight?"

"Enough." The sergeant grabbed Jacques by the arm and dragged him towards the young men now standing in six columns. "Get in line."

"Non!" Maman called out.

The sergeant turned on her angrily. "This man was

caught trying to escape," he said in broken French. "You should be glad we didn't shoot him."

"Contente?" Maman snapped. "You're tearing apart my life and stealing my home, and now I should be glad that you didn't shoot my son?"

The soldier swung his free arm and slapped her. Maman fell. He glared down at her. "I don't understand your gibberish," he growled. "But open your mouth again and it'll be the last time!"

"Laisse la tranquille!" Jacques struggled to pull away, but the soldier's grip was too strong to break. He swore loudly as the sergeant shoved him towards the line of Acadian men.

Jacques staggered. Hands reached out to hold him. "Steady now!" said a familiar voice, and Jacques glanced up into the face of his friend, Marc Tibou.

"You too?" he asked.

Marc shrugged. "My brother-in-law Pierre took off last week. The English haven't found him yet. I guess they want to make sure I don't join him."

"Do you know where he is?"

Marc shook his head. "Non, but…"

"Silence!" A young officer shouted in English. "Eyes front! Forward march!"

No one moved. The officer flushed as red as his tunic. He snarled an order at the guards, and they fastened their bayonets onto their rifles and waved them at the boys at the front of the line. The line started moving, heading towards the beach.

It wasn't a long march, but the boys moved slowly, their heads hanging in defeat. The women and children ran beside them, crying and calling out to them. Jacques walked tall and erect among them, refusing to even look at the soldiers prodding them along. I may be a prisoner, he thought, but I'm not giving up.

They were put into small boats and rowed out to the ships.

They were held prisoner there for more than a month. For the first few days, Jacques lay on a thin straw pallet in the hold, his stomach churning from the smell and motion of the ship. But the sea remained calm, and gradually he felt stronger. He began to spend his days on deck with Marc, watching the waves and talking. Their muttered conversations, full of plans of escape and revenge, eased the boredom of captivity.

Every morning, the soldiers rowed Maman and the other Acadian women out to the ships. The boys would devour the food and water they brought and ask eagerly for news. But there was little Maman could say; the men remained locked in the church, and the women continued to watch and wait.

More ships arrived in the harbour and dropped anchor.

"I've got to get out of here," Jacques exclaimed to his mother one morning as he helped her unpack her baskets. "I'm going crazy just sitting here waiting."

"How are you going to do that?" she asked sharply.

"Marc and I have talked to some of the others here," he whispered. "We've got a plan to escape."

"Non!" Maman's eyes widened with horror. "Didn't you hear what happened to François Hebert?"

Jacques shook his head.

"He escaped with some of his friends from one of the

other ships. The English caught him. They burned his parents' house down right in front of him."

Jacques groaned.

"And they promised to do the same to anyone else who tried to escape." Maman touched Jacques cheek gently. "Please Jacques, don't make it worse."

"Make it worse?" he shouted. "How can it be worse?"

Maman shook her head and tears filled her eyes. Jacques sighed. He put his arm around her shoulders. "Don't cry, Maman," he said.

Maman wiped her hand across her eyes. "I'm sorry," she said. "I'm just so worried. About you, Papa and Henri…and Étienne." She took a deep breath. "I didn't tell you before. But Papa is so discouraged. He honestly believed that Governor Lawrence would come to see reason. He thought that all this"—she waved her arm at the ships and the soldiers—"was just to scare us. All day he sits in the camp, sits and stares…"

"And Henri?"

"Henri's gone. To Port Royal. The English needed a blacksmith, and Luc Bourgeois—he's the blacksmith there; you know him." Jacques nodded. "He's disappeared. Ran off into the woods probably."

"And Anne?"

"She went with Henri. They're staying at his parents' house. I pray every day that they'll get back before…" She shuddered and turned away.

The next morning was warm and sunny. Jacques leaned against the wooden railing of the ship, studying the activity on the shore. The beach was crowded, and he could just make out teams of oxen pulling brightly-coloured carts.

"What do you think is happening?" he asked Marc.

"My maman told me yesterday that Winslow is planning to load everyone on the ships today," the other boy replied. "She said Winslow wants to keep families together. Papa was ordered to get them ready." Marc's father was the miller at Grand-Pré and, like Henri and Maman, spoke some English.

"How can they get everyone loaded in one day? It'll take ages to carry all their stuff."

Marc shook his head. "Each family is only allowed to bring what they need for the journey."

"What'll happen to everything else?"

"The English will take what they need, I guess, and send it to Halifax. The rest? Who knows?"

A loud cry echoed over the water and Jacques turned his attention back to the beach.

Blue-and-red-coated soldiers were forcing men, women and children into the small boats. Other soldiers were waiting with the oars to push off from the shore. Some of the Acadians tried to climb out and were roughly pushed back. Screams and cries filled the air as the boats began to move away from shore. Jacques swore angrily.

The first load reached his ship, and he joined the other boys in pulling the upset passengers onto the deck. Immediately he spotted Maman with baby Marguerite and Michel. He pushed his way over to them. "Where's Papa?" he asked.

Maman turned a tear-streaked face towards him. "I don't know," she said. "I climbed onto the boat and he passed the baby to me. When I sat down, he was gone. There were so many people, pushing and shoving and yelling…"

"I tried to find him," Michel's bottom lip trembled. "But there were so many people. Not just from Grand-Pré—from all over. The soldiers…" Michel shuddered. "I was afraid of losing Maman."

Jacques scowled at his brother. "So you left him there alone."

Maman touched his arm. "There was nothing we could do." A tear ran down her cheek. Jacques turned away. He stared towards the shore, straining his eyes for any sign of Papa.

An English soldier appeared in front of them. "That way!" He pointed towards the open hatch leading down into the hold. "Everyone's to go below decks. Now!"

"But there's no room," Jacques protested. The soldier swore. He grabbed Michel's arm and flung him towards the hole in the deck. "Below!" he shouted again.

Michel burst into tears. Maman dropped to her knees and wrapped her arms around him. Jacques cursed under his breath. He picked Marguerite up, settling her on his hip. "Come on!" he said, reaching his free hand down to his brother. "It's not so bad. We've been sleeping down there all month."

Michel continued to sob against Maman's shoulder. Jacques sighed. More boats were arriving and the crowd on deck was growing thicker. A heavyset young man stumbled against Jacques, knocking the baby. Marguerite shrieked and started to cry.

"Merde!" Jacques exploded. He grabbed Michel's arm and pulled him to his feet. "Stop acting like a baby! We've got to get down before all the space is gone!" He dragged his brother towards the hold.

Michel pulled away as they reached the top of the ladder. "I can go down myself," he said.

Jacques shook his head. "I'll go first with Marguerite," he said. "Then you and Maman. Go slowly and help her if you can." He tucked his little sister inside his jacket and smiled down at her. "Hold on tight," he said. Marguerite nodded, tears still glistening on her cheeks. Jacques placed his hand on the rickety wood and lowered himself down.

The ladder swayed alarmingly as he inched down step by step. Marguerite tightened her arms around his neck, almost choking him. The stench of hot sweaty bodies and fear hit him like a hammer, and his stomach lurched. He stumbled off the last rung. Placing the baby on the floor beside him, he turned to help Maman and Michel.

"It stinks down here," Michel whined.

"It's going to get worse," Jacques replied roughly. He gazed around, searching for a place to sit, but already the hold seethed with bodies. He picked Marguerite up and wrapped his arm around Maman's shoulder. He forced his way into the semi-darkness, Michel shuffling behind them. Voices grumbled and shouted as he pushed past, but he ignored them all.

The air grew darker and smellier as they moved into the hold. Finally, the press of people lessened, and Jacques spotted an opening beside some wooden barrels. He lowered Maman and Marguerite onto the floor and crouched beside them. Michel squeezed in next to them. "We can't stay here like this!" Michel said. "They're treating us like animals!"

"What did you expect?" Jacques snarled. "An inn?"

He wrapped his jacket around Maman. "Reste ici," he said. "I'll go look for Papa."

"I'll come too," Michel said. Together they threaded their way through the crowd, but a soldier blocked the bottom of the ladder. "Arrête!" he shouted awkwardly. "Asseyez-vous!"

"But my papa…" Michel started. The soldier snorted. "Your papa!" He waved his arm towards another boy. "His maman. Their sœurs. Everybody is looking for someone. Do you think I care?" He spat on the planks. "No one's allowed up."

Jacques didn't understand the words, but it was obvious the guard wasn't going to move. He pulled Michel to the side. "We'll wait here," he said. "We'll see him when he comes down the ladder."

The two boys waited. Neighbours and friends jostled each other as they stumbled down the ladder; soon there was no room to move. The air grew as hot as an oven. And still Papa didn't come.

"We'd better go back to check on Maman," Jacques said at last. "There is nothing we can do here."

They pushed their way towards the back of the hold, squeezing past arms and legs and bodies sprawled everywhere. Maman looked up eagerly, peering past Jacques into the darkness.

"He's not here." Exhaustion made his voice hard. "Maybe he was put on another ship."

"Non!" Maman pulled Marguerite against her chest. "Winslow promised. He promised to keep us together!" She closed her eyes and began to rock slowly back and forth. Jacques turned away. His chest was tight with rage.

He kicked a barrel hard. "I hate them!" he muttered. "I hate them!"

A sudden jolt almost knocked him to the floor. The wooden beams around him creaked and swayed. "They've cast off!" he shouted. A loud cry rose from the crowd around him. He pushed through the screams to the ladder. The soldier was gone. The hatch was closed but Jacques could see sunshine through the crack. He climbed up and put his ear against the cover. Outside English voices shouted orders, and heavy canvas flapped in the wind. He shoved at the hatch. It didn't budge. He put his shoulder against it and pushed with all his might. The crack opened slightly. Jacques wiped the sweat from his forehead and shoved again. The opening widened, and a blast of cold air made him gasp. He forced his arms and shoulders out and looked around.

Sailors were hauling on the thick ropes attached to the sails, pulling them taut before securing them with heavy knots. A large man held the wheel steady, while another took soundings over the side. But Jacques' attention was

caught by a huge plume of smoke darkening the sky. He wiggled out of the hole and slipped over to the railing.

His breath caught in his chest as he stared at the sight before him. All of Grand-Pré was on fire! Flames flickered up the side of the church, and black smoke billowed out of the community hall. Jacques strained his eyes, trying to see his house, but he couldn't make it out through the haze.

A hand touched his shoulder, and Jacques spun around, his fists swinging. His punch connected with something solid, and he heard a muffled gasp. He swung again blindly, but this time his wrists were trapped and held in a tight grasp. He struggled to get free. "Arrête!" A hoarse voice shouted in his ear.

Jacques froze. Slowly he raised his head. "Papa?"

"You've got a fist of iron there!" His father wiped the blood from his mouth. "I'm glad you're on my side!"

Jacques flung his arms around his father. "I didn't know," he said in a choked voice. "I thought it was... We looked everywhere..."

"Je sais," Papa said, hugging Jacques tightly.

"We were so afraid they put you on another ship." Jacques' voice broke. Just then, a loud crash echoed across the water. They jerked apart and stared at the flames on the shore.

"Probably a barn," Papa said hoarsely. A tear rolled down his cheek. "I didn't really think they would…"

"But they did." Jacques put his arm around Papa's shoulders. Together they stood and watched the dark smoke billowing up from their home.

Finally Papa took a deep breath. "But you're here!" he said. "And so am I!" He stopped. "What about the others?"

"Michel is with Maman and the baby in the hold."

"Dieu merci!" Papa said. "We're so lucky!"

"Lucky?" Jacques exploded in anger. "You must be crazy!"

But Papa shook his head. "We are lucky. At least we're together." He tightened his arm around his son. "Many, many people will be looking for their families tonight."

Jacques scowled. He stared across the water at the destruction. "I'll never forgive the English for this," he vowed angrily. "One day I will make them pay."

SEVEN
Boston

The cold wind bit through Jacques' coat as he leaned against the railing. The ship rocked heavily beneath his feet. Through the early morning fog he could see the outlines of the large fort at Castle Island guarding the entrance to Boston harbour.

Jacques straightened up, wiggling his shoulders to ease the stiffness in his back and neck. After months in the hold, with only short breaks like this on deck, he longed for open fields and the sweet smell of hay. He glanced at his mother, who was sitting on the deck, murmuring a soft lullaby to Marguerite. The little girl was restless and cranky with fever.

Jacques' fists clenched. He picked his way through the crowd of thin, sickly passengers to where Michel sat.

"Bienvenue à Boston!" he said bitterly. "What are we supposed to do here?"

"Live, I guess." Michel stared at the flickering lighthouse, his brown eyes as dull as his voice. "If we can. If they'll let us." He paused and nodded towards Marguerite. "She's worse, you know. Maman's worried."

Jacques glanced at his sister and his face softened. "So am I," he whispered. "She's had a rough trip."

Michel buried his head in his arms. "I couldn't stand it," he said hoarsely. "If she dies…"

Jacques crouched down and gripped his brother's shoulders. He forced cheer into his voice. "Don't worry. Marguerite is tough. Once we get off the ship…"

"If they let us land," Michel interrupted. He lifted his head and stared at Jacques. "Marc said his father heard some of the sailors talking yesterday. All the ships have to be examined before they're allowed into the harbour. For sickness." He dropped his head again. "We've got lots of sickness."

"They have to let us land." Jacques frowned. If they didn't…The Acadians had already been on board ship for several months with poor food and not enough water. Many were sick, and all of them were weak. If they were refused in Boston, most of them would die before the next port.

"I hate this wretched ship," Michel whined. "I hate sailing. I just want to get my feet back on dry land."

"On enemy land."

"I don't care. As long as it's solid."

Jacques dropped his hands and his voice hardened. "I'm not staying here," he said. "As soon as I can, I'm going back."

Michel jumped to his feet. "How?" he shouted. "How can you escape from here? Where would you go? Everything is gone, don't you understand?"

"We'll start over. Rebuild."

"It's not going to happen!" Michel yelled. Two men

standing at the railing turned curiously to stare at them, and Michel crouched down again beside his brother. "It's never going to happen," he said flatly. "We have to make a new life here."

"Never!"

Michel ignored him. "It won't be easy," he said. "But Papa's right—at least we're together." He repeated the words like a familiar litany.

"Except for Étienne and Henri and Anne," Jacques said. "Anne's baby will be born soon. Who'll be there to help her then?" He broke off abruptly. Leaning closer to Michel, he growled, "I'm not going to give up. No matter what it takes." He stood up and stalked away.

He paced the deck, pounding his fists against his sides as he walked. Papa and Michel are wrong, he insisted to himself. I know we're lucky to be together—I know that many families have lost husbands and children and wives. But the English have taken everything else. Our homes, our animals. I won't give up until I have it all back!

"Look!" Jacques spun around at the sudden shout. Michel was pointing towards the shore. "A boat's coming!"

Jacques ran to the railing and stared over the side. A wooden dory was battling the wind and waves. He watched as it inched up to the ship, and four men cautiously climbed the rope ladder to the deck.

Jacques studied the men. Two were dressed in rough seafarers' clothes; their hands and faces were tough and weather-beaten. They nodded to the captain and disappeared into the crew's quarters.

The other two were gentlemen. Their long frock coats and white wigs looked out of place on the ship, yet they moved with the grace of sailors who were used to the sea.

"Are they inspectors?" Michel asked.

"Maybe," Jacques said, "although they look more like merchants." He watched, puzzled, as one of the men drew out a document from his sleeve and passed it to the ship's captain. The captain read it and nodded.

The two men toured the ship. They inspected the crew's quarters and the galleys. They opened the hatch to the hold and peered down. One of the gentlemen took his handkerchief from his pocket and, holding it over his mouth and nose, climbed a couple of steps down the ladder. He was pale when he came back up. The two men studied the Acadians on the deck, and a flicker of pity warmed their faces.

Finally, the captain called Marc's father over, and the four men disappeared into the captain's quarters. Jacques paced the deck, waiting for them to come out. What would they decide? Would they turn the ship away? But when they finished talking with the captain, the two gentlemen didn't say anything to the Acadians. They called their oarsmen, climbed back into their boat and were rowed ashore.

Monsieur Tibou was surrounded immediately. Jacques wormed his way through the crowd until he could see the round face of the miller.

"They were sent by the government," Monsieur Tibou said. "They called it the Great and General Court. Apparently, the Court has told Lawrence they will not accept any more Acadians."

The crowd moaned.

"They've already let several ships land, but they were

in worse shape than ours. The people of Boston are worried about supporting us."

"What'll they do?" Jacques asked.

Marc's father shrugged. "They told the captain that they had to make a report to the Court. They were disturbed by our condition. They said they were going to recommend that Boston accept us." He shrugged again. "All we can do is wait."

The night passed slowly. Jacques sat in the hold, rocking Marguerite as his mother and brother slept exhausted beside him. Papa was on the deck, probably pacing and glaring at the darkness. As Jacques stroked the baby's hot forehead, his anger grew.

Word came late the next afternoon. The Great and General Court of Massachusetts granted permission for the Acadians to land. A weak cheer went up from the travel-weary people.

Jacques stood at the railing as the ship made its way into the inner harbour. The town rose above him, crowning the top of three large hills. Wharves ran out into the water, and church spires towered over the houses and warehouses.

"It's so big!" Jacques heard Maman say as he turned to see her staring across the water, Marguerite asleep against her shoulder.

"Oui," Jacques agreed. The town was larger than any place he'd ever seen. He had never even imagined so many houses, so many people in one place.

"Where will we go?" Maman's voice trembled. "How will we find our way?"

"Don't worry." Jacques struggled to keep his own voice

steady. He looked down, not wanting Maman to see her fear reflected in his eyes.

"At least we are together," Maman said.

Jacques nodded curtly and turned away, hot anger battling with dread inside him.

Not long after, the old and the sick were loaded into boats and sent ashore. Jacques and the others followed.

EIGHT

Mr. Thompson's Farm

Jacques pulled the blanket tight around his shoulders and wiggled closer to Michel. His brother was shivering, his lips blue with the cold. Maman's teeth were chattering as she huddled with Marguerite and Papa in the corner of the cart. The driver clucked softly to the horses; their heavy hooves clattered on the frozen road.

The countryside around them was dazzlingly white. Vast fields of snow sparkled in the winter sunlight. Lonely stands of maple and poplar stood black against the glare.

Marguerite whimpered. Maman lifted her into her lap. "Shhh, ma petite," she whispered. "We're almost there. We'll be at Mr. Thompson's farm soon." She held the little girl tighter. "Soon we'll be in our own little house."

An image of their cozy farmhouse in L'Acadie flashed across Jacques' mind, and he dipped his head to hide the sudden tears. When he looked up again, Maman was smiling sadly at him.

"I know," she said softly. "It won't be the same. But at least we'll be on solid ground, and not in Boston."

Jacques wiped his hand across his eyes and nodded. Maman had hated the port of Boston! They'd spent three weeks in the noisy town, squished together in a single house with two other Acadian families. The townspeople scowled at them whenever they went out, muttering under their breath about the dirty French Neutrals who had arrived uninvited, with no food or proper clothes.

"Look!" Michel jumped up and pointed across the field to a collection of buildings. "That has to be the farm. We're almost there!"

The driver was a sour-faced New Englander who didn't speak any French. He shot a cold look over his shoulder at Michel and slapped the horses with the reins. They lurched forward. Michel staggered and almost fell.

Jacques studied the buildings as they drew closer. Closest to the road was a small log house, its windows covered with oiled paper. There was no smoke curling out of the chimney and no sign of movement from inside. That'll be our house, he thought. The Thompson's house was set back farther, a narrow cart path winding up to it from the road. It was larger than the house Jacques would be sharing with his family, but it too was bare and simple. Glass windows were the only sign that Mr. Thompson wasn't poor.

The cart pulled up outside the log cabin. "Out you go!" said the driver, flapping his arms at his passengers. Papa climbed down and reached up for Marguerite. He settled the two-year-old's head on his shoulder. His hands shook as he helped Maman down. "She's worse," he whispered, holding the little girl close. Maman nodded, her eyes filling with tears.

Jacques and Michel jumped out of the cart and stamped their feet on the frozen ground. Jacques' toes ached as the blood began to flow again. They hobbled over to the house and threw open the door. Maman and Papa followed.

The cottage had two rooms. A large fireplace dominated the main living area, along with a well-scrubbed wooden table, a cupboard for their dishes, a bench and a couple of rough, handmade chairs. A doorway beside the hearth led into a tiny bedroom, where a wooden pallet was covered with a thin straw mattress and some heavy woollen blankets. Stairs led up to a small loft.

"Papa and I will share this room with Marguerite," Maman said. "You two can sleep upstairs."

A deep voice spoke from behind them. "I hope you'll be comfortable." They spun around to see a big beefy man standing in the doorway, a young teenaged girl behind him.

Papa bowed slightly. "English no," he said, shrugging his shoulders. Irritation flickered across the other man's face. He glanced at Jacques.

"My father no speak good English," Jacques said. "I learn a little in Boston."

"I speak a little too," Maman said, setting Marguerite on her feet, stroking her hair as the little girl stared at the stranger.

The other man nodded. He touched his chest. "I'm Mr. Thompson," he said. "And this is my daughter, Elizabeth."

Jacques looked at her intently. She was almost as tall as he was. She was wearing a plain grey dress and soft, leather boots, but her hands were rough and red. Under her bonnet her face was freckled. A tiny frown creased her forehead. Her blue-grey eyes gazed coldly at Jacques and his father.

Mr. Thompson hesitated. "We told the Selectmen we'd give you a house, and in return you'll work for me," he said. His words were stilted and formal.

Jacques translated, and Papa smiled. "Merci." He looked at his son. "Tell him that it'll be good to be on a farm again."

"Come on. I'll show you around," Mr. Thompson said. "Elizabeth, you stay and help get the family settled in."

Jacques followed the two men as they walked down the path. "My father built the log house when he first got this land," Mr. Thompson explained. "He lived there until he died two years ago." He pointed towards the big house. "I built this one when I got married."

Jacques struggled to translate his words to Papa. "Tell him it is a good house," Papa replied. "A strong house."

Jacques repeated his father's words reluctantly. Mr. Thompson nodded, then led them into the barn. It was dark and warm and smelled strongly of livestock and leather harnesses. A rush of homesickness swept through Jacques at the familiar scent. "This is where I keep my milk cows in the winter," Mr. Thompson said, waving his hand at the animals standing tied side by side. "And my oxen." He rubbed one of the heavy beasts between its eyes. Jacques noticed that his hands were as rough as his daughter's.

Jacques translated, and Papa replied in rapid French. "Papa asks what you grow?" Jacques asked.

"Corn and rye. We also have a small orchard for apples

and cherries." He stopped beside the last stall. "We have two horses. The mare over there…" He nodded vaguely towards the next stall, "and this beauty." He stroked the chestnut brown nose sticking over the door. "This one's young. He still has a lot to learn."

Papa reached over and patted the horse's strong neck. "Tell Mr. Thompson," he told his son, "thank you for what he is doing for us." Jacques scowled as he translated.

"I made an agreement," the farmer replied. His tone was hard. "I always keep my word. If you work hard, I'll make sure you have everything you need."

Papa's face turned red as Jacques repeated Mr. Thompson's words. "I'll do my best," he promised. Jacques' chest tightened with anger. His father's embarrassment was more than he could stand. Turning away abruptly, he stalked out of the barn, stomped past the shed and pigsty hiding in its shadow, and stopped at the edge of a field. It was cold and empty, covered with snow, but in the distance, Jacques could hear the roar of the sea. Just like at home, he thought. He struggled to breathe past the ache in his chest.

He gazed at the barren field for a long time, fighting tears. The wind blew through his thin jacket. At last his shivering drove him back to the log cabin. Thin smoke was coming out of the chimney. Michel was outside, chopping more firewood, but Jacques ignored him and flung open the door. He stopped in surprise. Elizabeth was sitting in one of the chairs, little Marguerite cuddled in her lap. She was rocking slightly, singing a lullaby in a soft voice.

Maman was bustling round, arranging their few possessions.

"Jacques!" Maman cried. "Come in and get warm!" She pulled him towards the fireplace. "Soon it'll be just like home!" She was smiling. The muscles along Jacques' jaw clenched, and he opened his mouth to yell, how can you say this place is like home? But with a jolt he understood. For the first time in months, Maman had her own kitchen, her own place to sleep. Tears leapt to his eyes again, but he blinked them away. Anger and homesickness seethed inside him.

"What's she doing here?" he muttered, glancing at Elizabeth.

"Looking after the baby." Maman smiled gently at the young girl. "Marguerite likes her."

Jacques' anger exploded. He spun around to face Elizabeth. "You steal my sister too?" he shouted in English.

"Jacques!" Maman grabbed his arm. "Arrête! She's helping me! Leave her alone." Elizabeth stood up and placed the child on the floor. "It's okay."

But Jacques couldn't stop. "You want take her?" he shouted. "Give her to your maman?"

Suddenly tears began to pour down Elizabeth's cheeks. She turned and ran out of the cottage.

Jacques looked at Maman. Her mouth was thin and disapproving. "Her mother's dead," she said. "Elizabeth told me. My English isn't good, but I understand enough. Her maman died when she was just a little girl." She picked Marguerite up from the floor with a sigh. The two-year-old began to whine. Maman carried her through into the tiny bedroom, and Jacques could hear her pacing back and forth across the room.

NINE

A Wild Ride

The dark, cold winter days dragged on. Marguerite grew worse. Elizabeth and Maman took turns rocking her as her face burned and she struggled to breathe. At last Mr. Thompson sent for the doctor, but there was little he could do. Jacques tiptoed around the cottage, his stomach in knots, or threw himself into the farm work, leaving the house before it was light and returning after dark. He avoided Elizabeth, and she refused to look at him whenever their paths crossed. Michel grew even quieter, hiding in the corner of the kitchen, carving little toys for his sister from pieces of wood. Finally, after they had been in the cottage almost two weeks, Marguerite's fever broke, and Maman began to smile again.

Then Papa got sick.

Jacques pushed open the door and stumbled inside, his arms full of firewood. He stamped the slush off his boots. "Mon Dieu, it's cold!" he said. "It sure doesn't feel like March." He looked across the room where Michel was sitting, whittling. "How is he?"

"Not good."

Jacques dropped the wood with a crash into the box beside the fireplace. "Mr. Thompson will have to send for the doctor."

"Pas encore." Maman spoke softly from the doorway of their bedroom. "The doctor is a good man," she said. "But doctors cost money, and Papa…"

"Papa what?"

Maman sighed. "He always worked so hard," she said. "He's ashamed to be living on charity."

"And he doesn't eat!" added Michel. "He slips his food to Marguerite—he doesn't think I notice, but I do!"

"If Mr. Thompson gave us enough he wouldn't have to!" Jacques said.

"He gives us what he can," Maman said. She closed her eyes and massaged her forehead. "But that's not the problem. Not really." She picked up a clay bowl from the table and put it into the cupboard. "He misses Henri and Anne, and he worries so much about Étienne." Her face crumpled. "I wish we would hear something, anything…"

Jacques looked away, embarrassed. "Papa just needs some rest, that's all," he said. "Michel and I can handle the farm work for now. Right, little brother?"

"Right!"

Maman forced a smile but didn't say anything. She wet a rag in the basin of water and began to wipe the table.

Jacques shifted his feet uncomfortably. "Michel, mon frère, why don't you start checking the harnesses?" he suggested. "See what needs to be fixed before ploughing starts. I'm going to ride over to the south pasture and have a look at the fences. Mr. Thompson is hoping to let the cows out to graze now that most of the snow is gone." He buttoned his jacket, glanced once at his mother, and went out.

The morning was sunny and clear. Frost covered the ground, sparkling in the bright sunshine. In contrast the barn was dark. Jacques saddled the brown mare. He was surprised to see that the stallion was already gone. He led his horse outside, mounted, and began to pick his way across the frozen field. The strong smell of the horse mixed with the fresh spring air. Jacques could almost pretend he was in Grand-Pré, trotting across his father's land to the Minas Basin.

Suddenly, the young chestnut appeared out of no-where, tearing across the field towards him. His ears were flattened against his head and his eyes were wild. Elizabeth leaned across his neck, her hands tangled in his mane. Jacques' laugh stopped in his throat when he saw the look of terror on the girl's face.

He urged the mare into a gallop, but she couldn't run fast enough to catch up with the panicked stallion.

Elizabeth lost her grip and fell. She hit the ground with a thud.

Jacques leaped from his horse. The ice cracked under his feet as he ran to her side. The girl lay still. Her breath was coming in short gasps, but her eyes were open, and she stared at Jacques.

Jacques knelt beside her. "All right?" he asked in his awkward English.

"I…I think so." Elizabeth struggled to sit up. "I don't think anything is broken."

Jacques put his arms around her. She leaned against

him, trying to steady her breathing. Her slender body felt warm and limp, like Marguerite after a temper tantrum. Jacques held her closer. Elizabeth stiffened and pulled away. Jacques flushed and jumped to his feet. He reached for her hand. "Come on," he said. "I'll take you home."

"No, thank you." Elizabeth ignored his hand. She gestured towards the spot where her horse had disappeared. "I have to catch him."

"Catch him?" Jacques shook his head. "He's too fast. You go home—I look for him." Elizabeth drew herself up haughtily. "I can do it myself."

"Okay!" Jacques shrugged. "Run after the stupid horse." He climbed onto the mare. "Maybe running more easy than riding!"

"Don't be rude!" Elizabeth's blue-grey eyes flashed. "I've been riding since I was a baby."

"So why you fall off?"

She scowled. "He got spooked. A crow flew up and…"

"Spooked?" Jacques frowned.

Elizabeth rolled her eyes. "Frightened. Scared. He's just young—he still isn't used to being ridden."

"So why you riding him?"

"To get him out of the barn and let him stretch his legs," she said. "Not that it's any of your business!"

Jacques grinned. "He stretch legs all right!" He patted the saddle behind him. "Come on. I give you a ride."

Elizabeth tossed her head. "I told you. I don't need your help," she said.

"Why not?"

"I don't take help from heretics!"

Anger blazed in Jacques' eyes. The Acadians had quickly learned the meaning of that word from the people of Boston. "I'm not heretic."

"Yes, you are. My father says your family prays to statues. That's what heretics do."

"We don't..."

"You do! And you want priests and Masses."

"We want..." Jacques flushed as he struggled to find the words. "We are Acadians... Catholics, and we want Mass, yes. Something wrong with that?"

"Yes!" Elizabeth shouted back. "You're in Massachusetts now!"

"So?"

"Things are different here! You have to try to fit in!"

"Never!"

Elizabeth took a deep breath and lowered her voice. "Then you'll always be foreigners, living on charity! The charity of hard-working Englishmen!"

Jacques tightened his hold on the reins to control his trembling. "Englishmen stole our home," he said, forcing the words through the fury in his chest. "We never want charity! We want to be left alone!"

Elizabeth picked up her torn skirts. "That doesn't change anything," she said. She limped away towards the house.

Jacques swore loudly in French at her retreating back. I won't forget this, he promised himself, as he turned the mare's head and urged it into a gallop. I won't forget.

TEN

A Visit from the Selectman

That night at supper, Papa pushed his empty plate away and leaned back in his chair. "Ah," he sighed. "A meal fit for a gentleman. I couldn't eat another bite."

"Now Bernard," Maman began. "Don't be like that. We have to be thankful."

"I know, I know," Papa said in a resigned voice. "We are lucky to have meat, even if it is from an old bull."

Jacques spit out a piece of tough, stringy meat, and pushed his chair away from the table. "I guess it was all the charity Mr. Thompson could afford," he said spitefully.

"Now, Jacques," Maman said, but he interrupted her.

"Je sais, je sais," he said. "He's been good to us. He's given us a home and food to eat. I'm just tired of depending on other people!"

Michel dropped his eyes, staring at the table in front of him.

Papa sighed. His face was haggard, lines of worry etched around his mouth and eyes.

Jacques longed to tell him what Elizabeth had said—

the insult still smarted. But he bit his tongue. "Sorry," he muttered.

The knock on the door startled them all.

Michel ran to the door and opened it. Mr. Davis, the town Selectman, stood there. "Evening," he said, twisting his black tricorne hat in his big hands. "May I come in?"

For a moment they all stared at the man. Mr. Davis had first come to see them in Boston. Like others chosen in towns around the countryside, he was responsible for the care of the French Neutrals, and especially for making sure they didn't become a burden on the people of Massachusetts. It was Mr. Davis who had arranged for their family to come to Mr. Thompson's farm.

Jacques scowled. What could the Selectman want now?

Maman jumped to her feet. "Bienvenue!" she said. "Come in. Drink?" she asked. "Ou souper?" She waved her hand towards the table.

Mr. Davis smoothed his silk waistcoat over his round stomach. "No thanks, Mistress," he said solemnly. "I just want to talk to your husband."

Maman nodded. She began to clear the dishes off the table. Papa pushed himself to his feet.

"Sit down." Mr. Davis waved Papa back to his seat and sat down beside Jacques. He placed his hat on the table in front of him. Michel slid onto the bench beside baby Marguerite.

"I heard that you were ill," Mr. Davis said.

"He tired," Jacques said quickly. "The boat…Acadia far away…"

Mr. Davis nodded but kept his eyes on Papa. "Does he understand?"

"A little," Jacques replied. "My English better." Speaking with Mr. Thompson every day had helped Jacques to learn and understand more words.

"Mr. Thompson said your father is not working," Mr. Davis said.

Papa looked at Jacques questioningly. Jacques translated the Selectman's words, and Papa's cheeks reddened. "Non," he replied, "mais peut-être demain…"

"Demain?"

"Tomorrow," Maman said. "Soon. He need rest." She took the kettle from the fire and poured water into an earthenware basin.

"Et meilleure nourriture," Jacques mumbled under his breath. Papa shot him a warning look.

"Michel and me work hard," Jacques said.

"Mr. Thompson told me that," Mr. Davis agreed. "But," he looked down and ran his fingers around the brim of his hat, "it's my duty to make sure that the town doesn't go into debt to support you."

Papa looked at Jacques, but he shrugged his shoulders. "I don't understand," Jacques said.

Mr. Davis looked up and sighed. "Just tell your Papa that I have a job for Michel."

"What?" Maman spun away from the dishes she was washing to stare at the Selectman. "But he works here…"

"It's not enough," Mr. Davis said roughly. "Mr. Giles needs a cabin boy. Un garçon cabine." He stumbled over the French words. "Mr. Giles is a trader."

"Trader?"

Mr. Davis' fists clenched, but his voice remained calm. "Un marchand. He makes trips from Boston to

Nova Scotia, and south to the Carolinas." He looked at Michel. "Your son is just the right age."

Jacques' heart leaped. He looked quickly at his brother. Michel's face was white, and his lip trembled, but he didn't say anything. Sissy! Jacques thought. This was it, an opportunity to escape. Once on the ship… "I'll go!" he said.

Mr. Davis shook his head. "You're too old for a cabin boy. Besides, you are needed here. Michel…"

"Non!" The plate Maman was drying crashed to the floor. "He's too young!"

"He's twelve, almost a man now." Mr. Davis looked at Maman and his face softened. "Mr. Giles is a good master. He's fair and he'll pay the boy well."

Papa stood up wearily. He looked at Jacques. "Tell Mr. Davis that I will go to work in the morning. Tell him please not to take my son."

Anger shot through Jacques like an arrow. That Papa had to beg this Englishman was almost more than he could take. He gripped the edge of the table to keep his hands from shaking and forced the words out.

"Sit down." Mr. Davis gestured towards the bench and Papa sank down. Mr. Davis spoke to Jacques. "Don't be foolish," he said. "Your father still needs rest. The lad needs work and Mr. Giles needs a cabin boy."

"My son not sailor," Maman tried desperately. "He's afraid." Her eyes pleaded with the Selectman. "We are farmers, not sailors. It make him sick."

"He'll survive." Mr. Davis stood and pulled on his hat. "I'll be back in two days for him. Be sure he's packed and ready to go." The door closed behind him.

Michel burst into tears. "I don't want to go, Maman,"

he sobbed. "I can't."

"I know, mon petit." Maman caressed his hair. "I know."

"Mon Dieu," Papa whispered. He covered his face with his hands. "Why can't they leave us in peace?"

Jacques jumped to his feet. He grabbed a mug from the wash stand and flung it at the wall. It hit with a thud. "Haven't they done enough?" he cried. "Our homes, our lands, our pride. Now even our families aren't safe! I told you we should have fought!"

Marguerite burst into tears at the noise. Maman picked her up and hid her face in her daughter's hair. Papa leaned forward and hid his face in his arms. Jacques bolted for the door.

"Jacques." Papa's voice was muffled. "Go and see Mr. Thompson. Perhaps he can help."

"What can he do?" Jacques pushed the door open. "He doesn't want us here—he'll probably be glad Michel is gone!"

Papa shook his head. "Non," he said. "Mr. Thompson is fair. He'll help us if he can."

Jacques spun around. "He calls us heretics and charity cases," he shouted. "Elizabeth told me! We can't ask him for help!"

Papa lifted his head and looked at his son. "We have no one else to turn to," he whispered. "He has to help. Now please, go!"

Jacques slammed the door behind him.

The night was crisp and cold. He stomped across the frozen ground and pounded on the door of the big house.

"Yes?" Elizabeth's voice was as icy as the night.

"Please. I need see your father."

"Come in. I'll get him."

Jacques had never been inside the Thompson house before. He looked around. Like their cabin, the door led into the kitchen. A huge fire crackled in the fireplace and reflected on the polished surface of the table. Strings of onions and spices hung from the ceiling, filling the room with a strong aroma. A spinning wheel dominated one corner.

A doorway led into the rest of the house. Mr. Thompson appeared in it, Elizabeth behind him.

"Good evening, Jacques." Mr. Thompson's weather-beaten face was puzzled. "How can I help you?"

"Mr. Davis… He wants Michel to work for Monsieur Giles. A…a cabin boy."

Mr. Thompson nodded but said nothing.

"He will die!" The words came out in a rush. "And Maman. She is sad, crying…" He bit his bottom lip then blurted, "Please help us."

Mr. Thompson nodded again. "Sit down," he said. "Elizabeth, bring us some cider." He scratched his head. "Let's see what we can do."

Jacques perched on the edge of the wooden bench.

"Michel is only twelve."

Mr. Thompson stayed standing, staring into the fire. "Mr. Davis is a fair man, but a stubborn one. It's not easy to make him change his mind." He smiled as Elizabeth handed him a mug of steaming cider. Jacques' hand brushed Elizabeth's as he took his cup and she jumped. Jacques flushed. Elizabeth wiped her hand on her skirt and sat down at the spinning wheel.

"Yes, Mr. Davis is fair," Mr. Thompson repeated. "He works hard for the good of us all." He took a sip of cider. "But sometimes with less compassion than is needed."

"Compassion?"

"Kindness."

"Oh… Can you help?"

"Maybe. I'll ride over tomorrow and talk to him. There'll be plenty of work for Michel here, especially when the planting begins. The other farmers will need help as well. I'm sure we can keep him busy. Still…" He paused. "Mr. Davis may not change his mind."

"And he says no?" Jacques clenched his fists. "What we can do?"

Mr. Thompson looked at Jacques. "You can petition the General Court."

"I don't understand."

Mr. Thompson sighed. "I wish you could speak English!" he said, then waved his hands as Jacques bristled. "Never mind…" He took a drink of cider. "You can ask the Court to help you."

"They not listen to us!"

"Don't be so sure. Many of the French Neutrals have already made petitions—asked for help." He took another sip. "The people of Massachusetts Bay believe in fairness and compassion for all."

Jacques didn't understand all the words, but Mr. Thompson sounded bitter.

"We didn't want you here," the farmer continued. "But now that you are, we are trying to do what is right for you."

"Even for heretics?"

Elizabeth's father turned to look at her. She blushed and stared at the floor. "My daughter isn't as careful with her tongue as she should be," Mr. Thompson replied. "But we believe God calls us to be fair to all men." He touched Jacques' arm. "We are not your enemies."

Oh yes, you are, Jacques thought. But who else was there? "Merci," he whispered. "Thank you for help." Without another word he left.

It was almost suppertime the next day when Mr. Thompson knocked on the cabin door. "I'm sorry," he said. "I went to speak to Selectman Davis, but he won't change his mind."

"Thank you. You tried." Maman said softly.

"It's not over yet," Mr. Thompson said. "We will petition the General Court. It may take a little while, but your son won't be gone for long."

"Thank you." Maman closed the door behind him. All night, Jacques sat up with his brother.

"I know I'm not brave like you or Étienne." Michel's voice quivered. "I never wanted to go away and fight. I just want to stay here with Maman and Papa."

"I know. It'll be all right. Mr. Thompson will help. Besides..." Jacques put his arm around Michel's trembling shoulders and lowered his voice. "This may be our big chance. Sailors hear things and see things that farmers don't. Maybe you'll hear something about Étienne or Anne and Henri. Or news from home." Jacques squeezed his shoulders. "Just keep your ears and eyes open. Maybe there's some way we can use your new job for our own good."

"I'll try, Jacques." Michel's brown eyes glistened with tears. "I'll try, but I'm so scared."

"I know." Jacques hugged his brother tighter. "Just remember—we're proud of you. You'll be a real man, earning your own way."

Michel nodded dumbly. He stared at the small bundle of clothes on the floor beside him. Just after dawn Mr. Davis appeared in a cart to take him away.

ELEVEN
Reunion

Jacques swung the hoe, digging deep into the black soil. The rich smell of newly-broken earth filled the warm spring air, and it made his heart ache. Just a year ago he had been working his father's farm. Now he was still digging up the land, but for an English master. Jacques' chest tightened. Someday soon, he promised himself. Soon.

It was almost two months since Michel had left. True to his word, Mr. Thompson had helped them to petition the Court. The Committee had sided with the Terriots and ordered the Selectmen to release Michel from his binding out. Unfortunately, Michel was already out at sea.

Jacques moved row by row across the garden. Sweat stung his eyes and poured down his back. Across the field, Papa laboured together with Mr. Thompson and some local men.

"Jacques! Hey, Jacques!"

Jacques' head jerked up in surprise. Elizabeth was running across the field towards him.

She stopped breathlessly beside him.

"What do you want?" he asked rudely.

The sparkle faded from Elizabeth's eyes. "Your mother sent me to find you," she said coldly. "She says to come quickly. You have visitors."

"Visitors? Who?"

"I don't know. We were in the yard washing the clothes when a wagon pulled up and a giant man jumped down. Your mother started hugging him and crying and shouting for you and your father." She shrugged. "So I came to get you."

A giant man? Henri? Could it be? Jacques' heart soared. "Tell Papa," he yelled at Elizabeth and ran towards the house.

He burst through the door of the cottage. Henri sat beside the fireplace, sucking on a long, clay pipe. He was thinner than Jacques remembered, and his face was lined and weary. But his arms were tanned and strong, and he leaped from the chair and clasped Jacques in a great bear hug.

"Henri!" Jacques flung his arms around his brother-in-law. "I can't believe it! Where have you been? Have you heard any news from Étienne?"

Henri laughed. "Lentement," he said, letting go of Jacques and sitting down again. "First say bonjour to your sister."

Jacques turned towards the table where Anne sat sipping a glass of cider. Like her husband, she looked smaller and sadder. Her dress was faded and patched. He leaned over and kissed her cheek. She wrapped her arms around his neck and held him tightly. Suddenly

Jacques pulled away. "The baby," he said excitedly. "Where is it? Is it in Maman's room? Is it a girl or a boy?"

Anne's face dropped. "Gently, Jacques," Henri said.

Jacques looked around in dismay. "What is it?" he demanded. "What happened?"

"The baby died," Anne said. "He wasn't strong enough. The journey and all the sickness…" Her eyes filled with tears.

"And not even a priest allowed to bury him properly," Henri said bitterly.

"Hush," said Maman, putting down the dish she was holding and going to her daughter. She laid her hand on Anne's shoulder. "It's over now. We're all together— that's what's important now. Maybe, in time…" Her voice trailed off. Anne nodded. Just then Papa rushed in and grabbed her in a fierce bear hug. The sad news was told again.

Papa swayed. Anne put her arm around his waist and eased him into a chair. He covered his face with his hands. "Is there no end to this suffering?" he moaned.

Maman put her hand on his shoulder. "Bernard," she said. "We should be grateful. At least we have Henri and Anne back with us, safe and whole." Maman said.

"Yes." Papa lifted his head and wiped a tear from his cheek. "That's a story we have to hear. But first, let's get our travellers something to eat."

Jacques barely nibbled at his food. He squirmed in his chair, watching as Henri dunked the heavy bread into his stew. When the bowl was wiped clean, he blurted, "Where were you? We asked everyone. Where did you go? How did you find us?"

Henri laughed. "One question at a time!" He paused to fill his pipe. "We've had our share of luck, I guess. But not at the beginning…" He blew out a soft cloud of smoke. "When Lawrence started rounding up the men, I was working at the fort near Port Royal. Anne was still on the farm with my parents." He frowned. "I wanted to rush back, but the English insisted that I finish the work. By the time I got back, they were gone."

"Where?"

Henri shrugged. "I didn't have a chance to ask, or even to look around. The day I got back to Port Royal, the English loaded us all on the ship."

"You weren't together?" Jacques looked at Anne. "How did you find each other?"

Papa laughed. "Maybe they can tell us," he said, "if you stop interrupting!"

"Pardon," he muttered.

Henri laughed too. "I thought…I prayed…that Anne was with my parents. I consoled myself with that thought for the entire journey. Otherwise I would've jumped into the water to find her." He smiled at his young wife. Anne blushed.

"My ship landed in Connecticut," Henri continued. "I met up with our old neighbour, Gabriel Dupruis. He said he saw Anne and my parents getting into a boat together. He didn't know where the ship was headed."

Henri drew on his pipe. Jacques chewed on his bottom lip.

"I didn't worry at first. I asked everyone I met if they'd seen them. Finally, I met Gabriel's cousin Daniel, who said they were on a ship that was sent to South Carolina.

Then I was worried! There was no way I could travel so far in this country. I didn't know my way around and I had no money. But I couldn't stop looking for her!

"Heureusement, I met a New England trader. He was sailing to the Carolinas and agreed to let me work for my passage. It was hard work on a cold and rough sea. When I finally reached South Carolina, I swore I'd never set foot in a boat again!"

"What did you do when you got there?" Jacques asked.

"When we docked, I began to ask everyone I saw, French or English! After two weeks of searching, I was almost crazy. But finally, I found Anne and my parents." He leaned over and tapped his pipe on the hearth. "We spent the rest of the winter in a house with another Acadian family. It was hard, especially after the baby died." His voice faltered. "But we made it."

"But how did you find us?" Papa asked.

Henri smiled. "God was looking after us, I think. The family we were staying with in Carolina heard from friends about a ship that had travelled from Grand-Pré to Massachusetts. We didn't know if you were on it, of course, but we had to start looking some place!"

"But how did you get here?" Jacques pushed his bowl away and leaned towards his brother-in-law.

Henri grimaced. "I broke my vow to myself! When the weather got warmer, I begged passage with another trader coming north. He agreed to carry Anne and our belongings in return for my labour on the ship. It was just as rough as the last time, and Anne was terribly seasick. But he brought us as far as Boston."

"Then we had more good luck," Anne said. "When we

arrived in Boston, we met Marc Tibou. He said you got off the ship there, but he didn't know where you had gone."

"He was on the same ship," confirmed Papa.

"Marc told us how to find the Selectman, Mr. Davis. And Mr. Davis told us where to find you! And here we are!"

"Dieu merci," said Papa. "You're here at last!"

Maman put her hand on Henri's shoulder. "And your Maman and Papa?" she asked softly.

Henri looked down and filled his pipe before he answered. "They decided to stay in South Carolina. They couldn't face another journey."

Papa sighed. "It must have been hard to leave them behind."

Henri nodded without speaking.

"We'll ask Mr. Davis to find you a place to stay near to us," Papa said.

"Ce serait bien," Henri said. "I have a strong back—I can earn our keep, as long as it doesn't mean any more boats!" He stood up and stretched. He picked a sliver of wood from the fireplace and lit his pipe. "Maintenant," he said. "How about you? How did you get here?" He looked around. "And where's Michel?"

"Our story is simpler than yours," Papa answered. "We arrived in Boston just after Christmas. We were sent here to Weymouth early in January. Mr. Thompson has been kind…" Jacques snorted, and his father glared at him. "It hasn't been too bad. At least we're in the country, on a farm…"

"Living on charity!" Jacques burst out. "Michel sent out to sea like a slave!"

Papa looked at his son. "Yes," he agreed. "We're living on charity, like all Acadians." He turned back to Henri. "Michel was bound out to a trader as a cabin boy." He hesitated. "I wasn't well, and Mr. Davis was afraid we would start costing Massachusetts money. But we petitioned the Court and we won! We expect Michel home again soon."

"And Étienne?"

"Nothing." Papa's face fell. "We've heard nothing."

"The English have declared war on the French."

"I heard," Papa whispered. "And somewhere my son is fighting beside a French soldier. I hope he finds what he is looking for."

"He will!" Jacques said. He thought of the last time he'd seen his brother. "And when the French win, we can join him. I wish we were there now!"

"Do you think you'd be welcomed by the French?" Henri asked.

"Of course. They're our brothers, our allies."

"I wonder." Henri began to fill his pipe again. "When I was passing through Boston, I met a friend. His brother's family had escaped from Massachusetts and gone to Canada. He claims they were robbed and abused by their French 'brothers.' They've petitioned the Great and General Court to be allowed back in the Common-wealth of Massachusetts."

"One incident doesn't prove anything," Jacques retorted.

"Peut-être pas." Henri nodded. "Still, I wouldn't be too fast to throw in with the French. They never helped us before. And they still have a mighty English force to defeat."

A knock on the door interrupted them. Elizabeth stood on the step.

"Come in," Maman said.

Elizabeth stepped inside and nodded to Anne and Henri. "Father asked me to welcome you both," she said. "If you want to stay, he'll talk to the Selectman about getting you work and lodgings. He'll be over to meet you later." She turned to go.

"Elizabeth?" Jacques called softly. She stopped but didn't turn as he walked up behind her. "Merci," he whispered. "Thank you. You come for me this afternoon. Henri et Anne...it was long, long time."

Elizabeth glanced over her shoulder at him. She nodded, turned and walked away without a word.

TWELVE

A New Conspiracy

Jacques dropped the bag of apples that he was carrying and wiped his sleeve across his face. The smell of the ripe fruit lay heavy in the hot August air. Voices rose and fell around him like the swarming of bees. A feeble breeze carried with it the distinct odour of the sea.

He stretched. Above him towered a tall weathervane. Jacques looked at it curiously. It was shaped like a giant grasshopper, staring down at the hustle and bustle of Boston's Faneuil Hall market.

"Hey, Jacques." Mr. Thompson's voice made Jacques jump. "I have some business to do while I'm here and Elizabeth wants to buy some cloth and household things. We won't be finished for a couple of hours yet. After you finish loading the cart, why don't you look for Michel? Mr. Davis said his ship is due in today. We'll bring him home with us."

"Thank you." Unwanted gratitude rose up in Jacques. "Maman will be glad to have him home," he said gruffly.

"Meet back here by three. I want to get an early start for home."

Jacques stowed the last bags of fruit, vegetables and flour in the wagon. He left the busy Boston market-place and wandered down King Street. Wooden shops and warehouses lined the road. Ahead he could see tall masts rising and falling on the water.

Mr. Giles, the merchant Michel had been forced to sail with, was a wealthy man. His warehouse was at the top of Long Wharf. Jacques pushed open the door and stepped into a small reception area. A young man with dark hair and a short woollen jacket sat on a stool behind a wooden counter. The tight cuffs of his shirt were stained with ink. He looked up from the heavy, leather-bound book in front of him and scowled.

"Bonjour," Jacques said. "I mean, good morning."

"We're not hiring," the clerk said, "especially not Frenchmen."

Jacques shook his head. "I'm looking for my brother, Michel. He was…"

"Useless!" the clerk interrupted. "That's what Mr. Giles said. Seasick the whole time!"

Jacques tensed. His English had improved during the months he'd spent in Massachusetts, and he couldn't miss the tone of disdain in the clerk's voice. "We warned Mr. Davis that Michel wasn't a sailor," he said.

"Waste of money, Mr. Giles said. But what do you expect from a dirty Frenchman!"

Jacques' right hand shot out and grabbed the clerk by the front his shirt. He dragged him across the counter and yelled into the young man's face. "Don't call him that!" He swung his fist, but a hand like iron gripped his arm. "Let him go!" a rough voice demanded.

Jacques loosened his hold on the clerk and spun towards the voice, his fist raised. The stranger blocked the blow, grabbed Jacques and shoved him against the wall. Jacques stumbled and fell.

The other man leaned down over him. He was short and stocky, and even the fine breeches and velvet jacket didn't hide his strength. "Now," he gasped. "Who are you and why are you attacking my clerk?"

Jacques looked up into the weather-beaten face and swore in French.

The strong man grabbed him and hauled him to his feet. "James," he said to the clerk. "Bring me some rope from my office and we'll tie him up until the Town Watch comes."

"Yes sir, Mr. Giles." The young man straightened his shirt and headed into the back room.

"No!" Jacques shouted, struggling against the man's grip. "Let me go."

"And why should I do that?"

"He insulted my brother."

"Your brother?"

"Michel. Your cabin boy. He called him a dirty Frenchman."

"So?" Mr. Giles pulled Jacques close and shouted into his face. "You people come here, live on our charity, and we have to put up with it." His spit sprayed Jacques' cheeks. "The Selectmen say we have to feed you and give you work. But they don't say we have to like you." He shoved Jacques away.

Jacques staggered; he clutched at the counter to keep from falling again.

"Your good-for-nothing brother cost me money—I had to pay him for doing nothing but puking over the side of the boat." He pointed toward the door. "Get out and take your filthy brother with you."

Jacques stormed outside onto Long Wharf. His cheeks were red and hot with humiliation and anger. He stomped over to the edge of pier and kicked one of the heavy mooring posts. He kicked it and kicked it until his muscles relaxed and the pounding in his head eased. Then he walked past the dories and small ships tied up at the dock, looking for his brother.

Around him men were loading and unloading cargo, shouting to one another in loud, rough voices. The smell of fish almost made him gag. His eyes were watering, and his breath was coming in gasps by the time he spotted Michel. The younger boy was climbing up a ladder from a dory, yelling in rapid French to another boy in the boat. Michel tied the thick rope securely to the post and turned. He grinned when he saw Jacques.

"Qu'est-ce que tu fais ici?" Michel cried. He threw his arms around his brother.

"Looking for you." Michel's excitement forced a laugh out of Jacques. He squeezed the younger boy tight against him. After a long moment, he held Michel out at arms' length.

"Well, you're not looking as bad as I expected," he said, still grinning. "Mr. Giles said you had a bad journey. You're all skin and bones, but nothing Maman's cooking won't cure."

Michel smiled. "I can't wait. I haven't had a proper meal in almost four months!"

Suddenly a face appeared on the ladder. "Are you going to leave me down here all day?"

Michel jumped. "Sorry, Jean," he said. "I forgot...my brother..."

Jean climbed onto the wharf. "Never mind," he said. "It's all fastened."

Jacques looked at him curiously. He was older than Michel, maybe his own age. "Who are you?" he asked. "Do you work for Mr. Giles too?"

The stranger shrugged. "Sometimes," he said. "I sail with Monsieur Giles from time to time, if business is slow at Greenough's."

"Jean was on this trip. For me, that was a good thing. He helped me. But mainly he works at Greenough's Shipyard," Michel whispered. "They actually build ships there. Jean's going to..."

"Not here!" Jean interrupted, glancing over his shoulder. "Let's go in Sam's—no one'll be able to hear us there."

"And I'll buy you a drink," Michel said, grinning. He touched the cloth bag fastened to his belt. "Mr. Giles paid me in coin."

Jacques smiled back. "A real man, earning his own money!" he said. Michel blushed.

The inside of Sam's Tavern was dark and warm. Low voices murmured across the heavy wooden tables. The smell of frying fish covered the stench from outside but did little to ease Jacques' stomach. He sipped at his cider and fought the nausea.

"My family's from Port Royal," Jean began. "I know your brother-in-law, Henri. Your sister was with us when we sailed on the ship to South Carolina."

"Anne and Henri are here now," Jacques interrupted.

Michel whooped. "When did they get here?" he asked. "Where are they staying?"

"They got here in the spring. They're staying at the farm next to us."

"What about…"

Jacques held up his hand. "Later," he said. "Let Jean talk first!"

Jean took a swig of cider. "The people of Carolina didn't want us," he continued. "They were only too happy to look the other way and let us go. My friends and I found work on a fishing schooner heading to Boston."

"That's what Henri did too," Jacques said. "I wish we could do it here. I'd be gone in a flash. But the General Court passed a law making it illegal to hire Acadians on the ships." He looked apologetically at Michel. "They passed it when you were already gone. Too many Acadians were trying to escape. Governor Shirley promised Lawrence he won't let the Acadians go back."

Jean nodded. "I know. But my friends and I have a plan. Soon we'll be heading for Louisbourg."

Jacques looked at Jean in amazement. "Where will you get the boat? How will you get out of the harbour?"

Jean stared into his cup. "We have a plan," he repeated. He looked up at Jacques and Michel. "You have each other," he said, his voice hard. "I have no family. My mother and sisters were put on another boat—I don't know where they were sent. And my Papa died on the ship. He died from smallpox and a broken heart." Jean clenched his teeth. "I'm going to fight!"

Jacques reached out and touched Jean's hand. "I know how you feel," he said in a low voice. "I want to escape and fight too!" His whisper was sharp and urgent. "Let me come with you."

Jean was silent. He looked at Jacques for a long time.

"Michel talked about you all the time we were at sea," Jean said at last. "Going on and on about his brother who tried to escape from Grand-Pré." His voice was taunting, but he ruffled Michel's hair with a grin.

"I would have gotten away if…" Jacques said hotly.

"I know." Jean's smile vanished. "Michel told me about your brother." He studied Jacques. "It was a brave thing you did, letting the English capture you so he could get away."

Jacques sat up a little straighter. "He's my brother. What else could I do?"

"Aren't you worried about being captured again?" Jean asked.

"I'll take the chance!" Jacques said intensely. "I spent more than a month in prison on that ship last time. I'd gladly spend twice that long, just for the chance." He banged his fist against the table. "I can't just sit here!"

Jean chewed his lip thoughtfully. "I'll have to talk to… I mean, I'll have to make arrangements…" he said at last.

"Merci."

Jean's dark eyes studied Jacques. "Go back to Weymouth with Michel," he said. "Pack what you need and meet me here in four days. Don't let anyone know where you're going." He flicked a glance at Michel. "And if you say a word…"

"You know me! I won't."

Jean drained his cider, his eyes never leaving Jacques' face. "I'll be here around six o'clock Wednesday evening. Don't be late."

Jacques bounced to his feet. "I'll be here!"

"If you're not," Jean said coldly, "we leave without you." He stood up and left the tavern without looking back.

THIRTEEN
Jean's Plot

Jacques wiggled out of the bed he shared with Michel and pulled on his faded trousers and a heavy woollen sweater. Clouds hid the moon and heavy rain drummed on the wooden roof. Jacques shivered. Rain again, he thought. Just my luck! His brother was still curled up, snoring gently. Jacques shook his shoulder and Michel jumped. He opened his mouth to speak, but Jacques put his finger on his lips.

"I have to go," he whispered.

"Now?" Michel propped himself up on his elbow. "Already? It doesn't take that long to walk into Boston."

"I have to go before Papa gets up," Jacques answered. "He'll never let me go."

"What will I tell him when he finds out you're gone? He'll blame me!"

"Non." Jacques shook his head. "Tell him you didn't know. Tell him I snuck away." Jacques forced a smile. "Tell him you thought I was going to the privy…"

His brother cocked his head, listening. "But it's pouring rain."

Jacques shrugged. "Je sais. But I can't wait. Jean will go without me."

"Even Jean can't sail in a storm."

"No, but he'll be ready. I don't know what his plans are, but he'll go as soon as he can. He won't miss the chance." Jacques squeezed Michel's shoulder through the blankets. "I can't either!"

Michel nodded as Jacques stumbled to his feet. "Take care, mon frère."

"You, too. I'll send news as soon as I can." He picked up his bag, which held a change of clothes, some food and the little money he had saved from helping Mr. Thompson at Faneuil Hall. He slung the pack on his back and pulled on his shabby deerskin jacket and leather boots. Without another word, he crept down the ladder.

The kitchen was pitch black. He could hear Maman and Papa's breathing from their room. Marguerite cried out softly in her sleep, but no one stirred. Jacques slipped out and closed the door behind him.

A great gust of wind almost blew him over. He pulled his cap tight over his ears. His boots sank in the mud as he inched his way forward. The blackness around him was complete. His clothes were drenched before he reached the road. The ground here was still slippery with mud, but Jacques could feel the firmness of the road through his boots. Using it as a guide, he headed towards Boston.

He met no one. He moved through the dark and the rain as unseen as a ghost. By dawn, he was barely a third of the way to Boston. The rain had stopped but thick clouds still hung like wet blankets across the sky. His legs burned with the effort of walking through the slippery mud. Hunger rumbled in his stomach and his hands were stiff with cold.

As soon as it was light enough to make out the shapes around him, Jacques headed towards a barn which lay close to the road. He tiptoed past the farm house, praying there were no dogs to raise the alarm. The heavy barn door creaked as he pushed into the warm darkness; a horse shifted nervously in its stall. Jacques paused, waiting for his eyes to adjust, and then crawled up the ladder into the loft. He made himself a nest in the straw and pulled off his coat and his boots. He dug in his bag for a sandwich. The rain had soaked through, making the bread soggy, but Jacques shoved the food into his mouth. A crunchy apple filled his mouth with sweetness. He savoured it, remembering the beautiful orchards in Grand-Pré. An ache washed over him, hardening into anger. They had no right! But soon he would get his revenge. He smiled at the thought. Curling up in the straw, Jacques closed his eyes and slept.

He awoke covered in sweat. The loft was as hot as an oven and thick with dust. Someone was moving in the barn below him, talking softly in English to the live-stock. Jacques lay still, hardly daring to breathe. After what seemed like hours, the farmer harnessed his horse and led it outside.

Jacques crawled to the edge of the loft and looked down. A couple of cows stared lazily up at him. No one else was there. Jacques grabbed his stuff and slipped down the ladder to the door. Through a crack, he saw that the rain had stopped. He watched as the farmer climbed up into a cart and moved off towards the road.

Jacques stretched, trying to work out the kinks in his shoulders and neck. He banged his boots against the wood of the stall, knocking clumps of mud onto the floor, and pulled them on. He slung his still-damp jacket over his shoulder and pushed open the door. After a quick glance around the yard, he ran towards the road. He heard a woman shout from the farmhouse, but he didn't stop until the barn was out of sight. Then he leaned against a tree and struggled to catch his breath.

The morning air was thin and grey. Jacques was surprised to see the pale sun so high in the sky—I must have slept longer than I'd planned, he thought. He pulled some bread and a piece of cheese from his bag and forced himself back into motion. Every step was an effort.

Sweat ran into his eyes. He legs felt like needles were sticking into him, and his shoulders were rubbed raw from the wet straps of his pack. But he continued on.

Faneuil Hall market was slowly emptying by the time Jacques reached it. People dragged themselves at a snail's pace through the humid air. The stench from the wharves was almost unbearable. Jacques tried not to breathe as he made his way towards Sam's Tavern. Jean wasn't there. In spite of the heat and the smell, Jacques forced himself to walk down Long Wharf to look for him. He was nowhere to be seen.

Jacques swore under his breath. He limped back to the tavern and sat down in the shade outside. He stretched out his aching legs. His throat was dry, but he didn't want to spend the small amount of money he had. I'll need it when I get to Louisbourg, he thought, until I make my first pay. He found an apple in his bag and bit into it; the juice stung his lips but made it easier to swallow.

He'd just finished the apple and stood up when Jean slipped around the corner of the tavern. "Bonjour!" he said softly. "You made it!"

"I had to make it."

Jean nodded. "We're going tonight," he said. "If the weather holds." He scowled at the sky. "They don't want to be on the sea in a storm."

"They?"

Jean shook his head. "I can't tell you anything else. There are too many ears around. All you need to know is that we're going tonight." He touched Jacques' arm. "There are still things I have to do. Meet me here at ten." He turned.

"I'll be here."

"And keep your head down." Jean vanished around the corner.

Jacques picked up his pack and put it on, excitement growing like a weed inside him. The church bells rang six times. Four hours to go! he thought. Then I'll be on my way. To fight. To join Étienne. The thought of his brother filled him with an urgent eagerness. He ducked around the corner and smacked into a short round man coming out of the tavern.

"Oh, excusez-moi!" he blurted. "I'm sorry!"

"Jacques?"

Jacques' head jerked up. He was face-to-face with Mr. Davis.

"What are you doing here?" The Selectman frowned. "You're a long way from home, aren't you?"

Home? Jacques stared at him. Home was Acadia, where the fields of wheat would just be turning golden. But of course, Mr. Davis didn't mean that. He meant Mr. Thompson's house. He meant exile in Weymouth.

Jacques bit his tongue to keep from shouting. He had to be careful, very careful. "Answer me," Mr. Davis ordered. "Are you here alone?"

"Yes. I...I come to see my cousin," he lied.

"You're supposed to ask permission to leave your area." Mr. Davis' voice was stern. "That's the law."

"Yes sir." Jacques nodded humbly. "But my cousin was sick, and Maman was worried. So I came as quickly as I could."

"Hmm." Mr. Davis was still frowning. "I didn't know you had relatives in Boston."

Jacques swore silently. "He's not really my cousin," he said. "We were neighbours in Grand-Pré. He got separated from his parents during the derangement."

"Will you be here long?"

"A day, maybe two." Jacques stared at the ground. "Gabriel should be well enough by then."

"Very well." Mr. Davis nodded. "I'll make out a permission slip for you. Come by my office tomorrow morning."

"Yes, sir," he replied meekly.

"And don't forget," Mr. Davis put his hand on Jacques' shoulder. "You'll have to go home no later than Saturday. It is a grave offense to travel on the Sabbath."

"Yes sir." Jacques felt a pang of guilt. He had broken the law, and the Selectman could have turned him over to the Town Watch. Instead, he'd agreed to help. But Jacques shook off the feeling. By Sunday he would be well on his way to Louisbourg. "Thank you, sir." he said.

"Stay out of trouble."

Jacques nodded, keeping his eyes lowered. He watched Mr. Davis stride down the street towards the shops. Jean will be furious, he thought. I better find some place to lie low until it's time to go.

Jacques wandered up King Street to the Town Commons. The green of the Commons spread almost as far as he could see. Off to his left some cattle grazed, unconcerned with the militia practice going on across the field from them. High on Beacon Hill Jacques could just make out the outlines of a large manor house.

Jacques wandered as close as he dared to the British militia and flopped to the ground. His legs still ached from the long walk into town. He studied the militia intently; they marched smartly, their muskets black in the sunshine. Jacques clenched his fists, remembering other men just like these setting fire to his home in Grand-Pré. The smoke had turned a crisp autumn day into darkness. He forced his anger down and struggled to concentrate. Any information he could get about the enemy would be useful.

But it was hot, the grass was soft beneath him, and Jacques was bone-tired. He fell asleep.

When he awoke, it was dark. The stifling heat of the day had eased, but the sky was black with clouds. Jacques began the long walk down King Street just as church bells rang the hour. Nine o'clock.

Jacques stopped outside Sam's Tavern. Loud voices and laughter drifted out. I'll wait out here, he decided. Mr. Davis might have believed his lie, but he didn't want to run into anyone else. He paced back and forth in the shadow of the building, drumming his fists against his sides.

The waiting seemed interminable. After ten minutes of pacing, Jacques flung himself on the ground and closed his eyes. Suddenly an image of Étienne flashed though his mind. His brother was dancing at Anne's wedding, stomping his feet to a lively fiddle tune, his face bright with laughter. Jacques' breath caught in his chest. We were so happy then. We thought life would go on like that forever.

At last, the bells chimed ten o'clock. Jean appeared out of the dark and gestured to Jacques. Two other boys were with him.

"Good! You're here." Jean gestured towards his companions. "This is Denis and Joseph d'Entremont. They're from Port Royal too."

"Bonjour," Jacques whispered. He could not see their faces, but through the dark he could sense their doubt.

"Come on." Jean's whisper was firm and strong. "Our boat's down at Greenough's Shipyard. Follow me, and don't say a word."

Jacques dropped silently into line. They moved soundlessly up King Street to Cornhill, and then headed back towards the water. The smell of salt and fish became stronger and Jacques could hear the lapping of the waves. Large wooden warehouses rose up beside him, and the skeletons of ships lay naked in some of the yards. It was unfamiliar territory to Jacques, but Jean and his companions moved comfortably and without hesitation.

The road sloped downhill, making the walk easier. They reached the gate outside Greenough's in just a few minutes. The paint was peeling on the dingy sign and the wooden fence was old and rickety.

Jean stopped. "Wait here," he said. He slipped through the gate. Jacques strained his eyes as his new friend ran towards a large, barn-like building. "The warehouse," Joseph whispered in his ear. "Our supplies are hidden behind it."

"How?"

"There are piles all over the yard, covered with canvas," Denis explained. "Half-built boats. Wooden kegs." He shrugged. "We just added one more." He winked at Joseph, and the two brothers grinned.

Jacques scanned the yard nervously. "Why aren't there any guards?"

"Greenough depends on the Town Watch to protect him," Joseph replied. "They make regular patrols, but they look after all the businesses in town. We have time."

Jean appeared at the corner of the warehouse and waved.

"Let's go," Denis whispered. They crept past the gate and into the shadows of the building. From the corner of the warehouse Jacques could see a small, single-mast ship lying at anchor not far from the end of the dock. "Voilà!" Joseph said. "Our passage to Louisbourg!"

Jacques frowned. "What do you mean?" he asked. "We can't ask for work—I told you Acadians aren't allowed…"

"Quiet!" Jean snapped. "We're not looking for work!"

He lowered his voice. "We're going to stowaway. This ship is carrying rye and molasses to Nova Scotia. If we can hide on board, we can make it to Halifax. Maybe closer."

"How do you know where it is headed?"

"We work here. People talk." Jean shrugged. "We listen."

"Won't it be guarded?"

"There's only one guard—the rest of the crew are on shore."

Jacques nodded. "Four against one—we can do it."

Jean shook his head. "We don't have to fight our way on board. The guard is a friend. He agreed to let us on board."

"Why?"

Jean looked at Jacques. "Not all the English hate us," he said. "Some of them hate what was done to us."

Jacques shook his head. "I don't trust any Englishman!" he said. He stared around, his eyes straining to see in the darkness.

"Then stay here!" retorted Jean. He nodded at the two brothers, and Denis and Joseph disappeared behind the warehouse. Minutes later they reappeared, dragging a heavy bundle between them. They pulled it to the edge of the pier, and untied it, revealing packages of food wrapped in oilskin.

"Where did you get all this?" Jacques asked in amazement.

"Mr. Greenough often hired us out to help the ships unload. While we helped the traders, we helped ourselves a bit too."

Jacques gasped. "You can be hanged for that!"

"They'd have to catch us first!" Jean trotted over to join the other boys from Port Royal.

Jacques stood frozen with indecision. He watched as they carried wooden casks of water from behind the warehouse and placed them beside the food. Jean ran back and returned with a length of heavy canvas. The three boys from Port Royal whispered together for a moment. Denis and Joseph nodded. Denis swung his legs over the edge of the wharf and disappeared down a ladder. They must have a dory there, Jacques thought. They're going to load it up and row out to the ship. He watched as Joseph followed his brother down the ladder, stopping with only his head visible over the side of the wharf.

Jean walked slowly back to Jacques. "We've done all the planning and all the work," he said coldly. "For Henri's sake, I'll ask you again—are you coming? Or are you going back to Weymouth to live on charity?"

The sarcasm in his voice stung Jacques into action. He glared at Jean and stomped over to the pile of supplies. He grabbed a barrel of water and lowered it down to Joseph. Jean smiled.

It was hard work. Jacques' legs quivered and his back ached. Denis loaded and packed the dinghy as quickly as they passed him the bundles. When they were finished, the small boat was full.

"It'll be a tight squeeze," said Jean. "Denis, you and Joseph row over to the ship. Unload the supplies and come back for us. Joseph can get everything stashed on board."

Denis nodded.

"Do you remember the password?"

Denis grinned. "L'Acadie toujours!"

"L'Acadie toujours!" Jean echoed as Joseph wiggled his way onto the dory. They picked up the oars and began to move away from the wharf.

Just then they heard a shout. Swinging around, Jacques and Jean spied lanterns hurrying toward them.

"Town Watch!" wailed Jean. "Run!"

Jacques fled. He ran to the shelter of the buildings and stopped, gasping. Behind him he could see Denis and Joseph rowing frantically towards the ship. One of the watchmen shouted, and an answering shout came from the deck of the ship. The two boys froze.

There was no sign of Jean.

Jacques heard the Town Watch calling for reinforcements. He crept through the shipyard, slipping from shadow to shadow, until he reached the corner beside the road. A quick glance confirmed no one was in sight. He scrambled over the fence. With the dullness of failure gripping his stomach, he headed back towards the town.

There's nothing I can do, he thought. If I go back, I'll get arrested. I'll get put in jail— maybe even worse! Jean will understand.

It was completely dark. The air had cooled, and a fine rain was falling. Jacques trudged up the hill to the Commons. He had nowhere to go. He had almost no money and no friends. He walked until he came to a livery stable. Inside, he curled up in an empty stall and fell asleep.

"Hey you!" Rough hands pulled him from his sleep. "What do you think you are doing here?"

Jacques opened his eyes to see a man as rough as his hands. Anger ran like a scar across his face.

"I, uh, got lost," Jacques said. "I needed a place to stay…"

"I ain't running no inn here." He lifted Jacques from the floor. "Get outta here before I call the Watch." He gave Jacques a violent shove out the door.

Jacques landed in a mud puddle the size of a small lake. Rain pounded onto the ground beside him. He got shakily to his feet. Around him the town was coming to life, but no sun penetrated the angry clouds overhead. Heavy with despair Jacques trudged towards the marketplace.

The square at Faneuil Hall was deserted. His hopes of finding a ride to Weymouth vanished. Hugging his coat tightly around himself, he began the long walk back to the Thompson farm.

FOURTEEN
Fire!

Jacques returned to Weymouth defeated. When Mr. Thompson asked where he had been, he retold the lie about his sick cousin. Maman and Papa said little; they were afraid that Jacques would be arrested if the truth was told. Jacques refused to tell them anything more. He just shook his head and muttered, "Quelle différence ça fait?"

Throughout the rest of the summer and into the autumn he worked on the farm, oblivious to the wonders around him. He didn't feel the heat of the sun or see the blazing fall colours. He didn't smile at Marguerite as she toddled through the towering corn or rolled in the blanket of fallen leaves. He swung his axe like he was wooden himself. Maman's joy at having Henri and Anne living on the neighbouring farm, Papa's improved health, even the announcement that Anne was once again pregnant failed to touch him.

He remained closed and empty; alone.

One afternoon, late in September, Jacques was working in the cornfield. The sun beat down on him, and his hands were cut and sore from twisting the corn husks off the stalk. He flung the ears of corn into the wagon and wiped his arm across his sweaty forehead. Papa and Henri stood beside the oxen, resting and talking.

"I heard that the government in Nova Scotia is starting to allow Acadians back." Henri's voice was full of excitement. "Maybe we can go back, start over."

"Start over where?" Papa asked. "There's no place to go. Nova Scotia's not Acadia. The English destroyed that along with our homes."

Jacques stared at his father, surprised by his bitterness.

"I saw it," Papa continued. "I saw the flames…" His voice caught. He wiped his sleeve across his eyes and shuffled back into the cornfield.

Jacques turned his back, trying not to see Papa's tears, trying not to remember the autumn day turning black as clouds of smoke billowed out over the fields. The memories were so vivid, he could even smell the smoke…

Jacques' head jerked up. Thick black plumes were rising from Mr. Thompson's barn. A strange, fierce joy filled his chest. Yes! he thought, at last an Englishman will know what it was like to suffer! To lose everything! Then images flashed through his mind—Mr. Thompson writing the petition to the Great and General Court, Maman singing in her new home, Elizabeth cradling Marguerite in her arms, the baby smiling up at her.

For just a moment, Jacques stood motionless, torn between his hatred of all things English and his gratitude to Mr. Thompson. Then he shouted to Papa and Henri and raced towards the barn.

Mr. Thompson was already there; Jacques could hear his voice in the barn, shooing the cows out. Jacques ran to the door, standing to the side to avoid being trampled by the panicked animals. Mr. Thompson staggered out, coughing and gagging. Jacques ran to help him, but the farmer gestured inside. "The stallion," he gasped. Jacques filled his lungs with fresh air and dashed inside. His eyes smarted and the hair on his arms shrivelled. The horse was slamming its hooves against the wooden stall, its eyes white with terror. Jacques reached for the rope halter, but the frightened animal tossed its head.

"It's okay, boy." Jacques spoke softly. He pulled off his jacket and flung it over the horse's head. The stallion paused, and Jacques lunged for the rope. Tucking it firmly under his arm, he struggled to untie the knots. His eyes swam with tears, and his lungs burned. The knots slipped in his sweaty hands. He bit his lip, forcing himself to stay calm. Finally, the rope came loose. He pushed open the stall and staggered towards the door, the quivering stallion close behind.

The sun hit his eyes like a flash of lightning, and he stumbled. Mr. Thompson caught him and eased the rope out of his hands. "Sit down," he said. He shouted across the yard to his daughter. "Elizabeth, bring Jacques some water."

She ran to the well and lowered the bucket. Grabbing the cracked wooden ladle, she filled it with cold water and raced over to Jacques. He gulped the icy water as tears poured down his cheeks.

With a loud crash, the roof of the barn collapsed. Sparks shot into the air.

"Take the horse up into the pasture," Mr. Thompson said to his daughter. "Then fetch Michel or some of the men to help drive the cows into the field as well. I'll get Jacques into the house."

"Non." Jacques said in a whisper. "I'm okay." He splashed some of the water on his face and laid his cold hands against his eyes for a moment. Then he climbed shakily to his feet and looked around.

Everything was blurry, but he could make out that the farmyard was flooding with friends and neighbours. Henri and several other men were attacking the ground with shovels, digging a ditch between the barn and the main house. Papa and some others were filling cloth sacks with dirt, laying them along the edge of the trench to reinforce it. Maman and Anne struggled with buckets of water, drenching the bags. Marguerite held hands with another girl not much older than she was, frowning intently as they stamped out the sparks that jumped the line. Thick smoke hung everywhere.

Jacques took a couple of shallow breaths, forcing the air past the searing pain in his chest. Turning away from Mr. Thompson, he grabbed a shovel and joined Henri. He cursed as an ember dropped on his arm. He rubbed the burn, but he didn't falter.

The defences held. The barn burned for hours, crackling like a demon. But the house was safe. One by one the workers left for home and supper.

Jacques sank down on the steps of the big house, breathing deeply the cool evening air brought in by the wind. Elizabeth handed him a glass of cider and he drained it in a single gulp. He glanced at her. She was staring at the debris as if she wanted to cry.

"I'm sorry." Jacques' voice rasped like sandpaper in his throat.

Elizabeth sniffled. "My mother loved that barn," she said. "She said it was so peaceful. She'd go out to do the milking, pat all the animals…"

"What happened to her?"

"She got sick…" A sob rose in her throat, choking her. She turned her head away so he wouldn't see the tears running down her cheeks.

Jacques hesitated. "The English burned our homes in Grand-Pré," he whispered.

Elizabeth took a deep breath. "I know," she said, not looking at him. "That wasn't right. I'm sorry."

They sat in silence, staring at the mess around them.

"Elizabeth," Mr. Thompson called across the yard. "Could you make us all something to eat? We can't let such good neighbours go home hungry."

Elizabeth struggled to her feet. As she turned to go, she whispered, "Thank you." This time Jacques nodded.

He got up and wandered towards their cabin. His stomach was queasy, and he could barely drag his feet up the steps to the loft. Stretching out on his bed, he fell asleep. He didn't even stir when Michel crawled in beside him.

He woke suddenly. His back was warm where Michel pressed against him. He lay still, wondering what had awakened him. He was just fading back into sleep when he heard it again. Hoof beats.

He climbed down the ladder and went outside. Smoke still hung like a shroud over the place where the barn had stood, but the sky over the fields was bright with moonlight. Jacques listened. The hoof beats were clear now, slightly off beat in the silence. They were coming toward him.

Jacques waited.

Soon he could see a dark shadow moving slowly up the road. The horse trotted cautiously, as if fearful of the ground. Its rider was slumped in the saddle, his head forward, as though he were sleeping. As Jacques watched, the rider began to slide sideways.

He ran and caught the figure just as he was about to hit the ground. A tremor of pain ran through the rider. Jacques tightened his grip and began to drag him towards the house.

"Wait," the man whispered hoarsely. "I can walk."

Jacques almost dropped him in surprise. Despite the weakness and pain in it, there was no mistaking the voice.

"Étienne!" He lowered his brother carefully into a sitting position and crouched beside him. "What are you doing here?"

"Jacques!" Étienne smiled feebly. "I could ask you the same question!"

"I heard your horse." Jacques stared, his eyes wide in amazement. "But how? Why?"

"Not now." Étienne shook his head and winced at the pain.

"Oh Étienne." Tears leaped to Jacques' eyes as he looked at his brother. In the moonlight he could see Étienne's cloak was tattered and marked with black spots which had to be blood. His face was drawn, and he held his right arm tight against his body. "You're hurt."

"Just a scratch." Étienne tried to smile again. "But that silly nag just about killed me!"

"Come on," Jacques said. "I'll help you into the house." He pulled Étienne up and held him against his side. They shuffled towards the cottage.

"Papa!" Jacques called as he pushed open the door. "Come quick! Étienne is here!"

Papa dashed out of his room, his arms flung wide in welcome. His broad grin collapsed when he saw his son. Without a word, he settled Étienne onto the chair and took off his blood-stained cloak. He tore the sleeve of Étienne's ragged shirt and stared at the arm in dismay. The wound was red and swollen. Pus leaked out like tears. Jacques' stomach heaved.

There was a small gasp from the bedroom. Maman stood in the doorway, her hands over her mouth.

Étienne forced a smile. "Just a scratch," he repeated. "The soldier wanted more than my arm!" He winced when Papa touched him.

"Jacques," Papa's voice was shaking. "Light the fire so Maman can heat some water. Then run to Mr. Thompson and ask him to send for the doctor. Michel, tether the horse and go get Henri."

Jacques flew up the hill to Mr. Thompson's house. He blurted out his request and tore back to the cottage. He found Étienne out cold on a make-shift bed beside the fire.

For three days, Étienne lay between life and death. His body burned with fever, and he cried in his sleep like a little boy. The doctor cleaned his wound, wrapped it, and said the rest was in God's hands. Jacques left his side only to do his chores and rushed back to wipe the sweat off his face and hold his trembling hand.

Finally, the fever broke, his breathing eased, and he was able to sit up and sip at some broth Maman made for him. But it was almost a week before he could tell his story.

He sat, wrapped in a wool blanket, beside the fire with Papa, Jacques and Henri. A jug of cider sat on the floor between them. Michel perched next to them on a stool, whittling.

Maman and Anne sat at the kitchen table, their hands busy with a quilt, but listening closely.

Étienne smiled slowly at his family. Jacques quivered with impatience.

"I didn't think I'd ever make it here," Étienne said at last. "I heard you were here in Weymouth from a friend, who heard from a friend…" He shifted slightly and grimaced at the pain in his arm. "But I never thought I'd make it home."

"Home?" Jacques cried. "This isn't home. Acadia is home."

"Non, Jacques." Étienne shook his head. "Home is where your family is." His voice was barely a whisper. "L'Acadie is lost. Lawrence gave our farms away to a bunch of Scotsmen."

"But Lawrence is letting Acadians go home!" Henri protested.

"Back to Nova Scotia. Maybe. But to Acadia—never."

"Then we have to fight," Jacques said.

"Non!" The word burst from Étienne like a bullet. "Look at me! Do you really think fighting is the answer?"

Jacques stared into Étienne's face. His brother's eyes were filled with pain. And something else. Darkness. Desperation. Defeat.

"You've given in!" he shouted.

Étienne sighed. "So much has happened since the last time I saw you," he said, speaking directly to his brother. "After I ran away…after I left you with those filthy

English soldiers…" His eyes were full of remorse. "I had to run. I didn't want to, but I knew you hadn't committed any crime. They would have hanged me for murder."

Jacques nodded.

"I went to Halifax and got a job as a deckhand," Étienne continued. "No one at the docks asked questions. I worked hard and kept my mouth shut. As soon as I could, I got passage to Québec on a ship sailing up the St. Lawrence."

He closed his eyes and struggled to take a deep breath. "I volunteered to join the French army. At first, they laughed at me, taunted me because I was Acadian. They didn't trust me."

"But you're French!"

"To the French in Canada we are cowards or English allies or both. Not worth their efforts." Étienne said bitterly. "But then war was declared, and the army needed every soldier it could get. Even dirty Acadians. The French enlisted me.

"I served as well as I could. I always got the worst jobs, the details no one else wanted. I was always reminded that I didn't belong." Étienne's voice rose. "But it didn't matter. I was where I wanted to be. Fighting the English!" He sighed. "I thought that was enough!"

"But?" Papa prompted gently.

Étienne threw a sharp glance at his father. "I went with General Montcalm and his army to Oswego," he said. "There were French regulars along with some militiamen from Canada. We were joined by some Indians who said they were French allies." His voice settled into a sing-song rhythm, as though it was a story he had told many times before. "It was a long hike south from Québec. There were three forts there, but the English had already abandoned the first two. Taking the third one, Oswego, was supposed to be très facile." He shifted his weight, trying to get comfortable.

"The battle was everything I dreamed it would be! We were all wild with excitement—the militia rushing in, the Indians were whooping their war cries, and the musket fire was deafening. I lost track of time—loading and reloading my musket, slashing with my bayonet…" Étienne's eyes glittered. "Then suddenly I was on the ground, with a hole the size of a fist in my arm."

"What did you do?" cried Michel.

"I crawled under a cart to hide." He shuddered. "The battle looked so different from there! All of a sudden, the soldiers looked like wild animals, tearing each other apart. Bodies were just left where they fell. And the blood…" Étienne scrubbed at his face with his hands. "It was horrible. The moaning of the wounded nearly drove me crazy! I passed out." Étienne's hand shook as he poured himself a cup of cider.

"When I came to," he said at last, "I was being half-dragged, half-carried. The sun was going down. The English had surrendered. There was a lot of cheering." Étienne took a drink and wiped his hand across his mouth. "I didn't cheer. I felt sick and angry. But that wasn't the worst of it." Étienne shuddered again.

Papa stood up and put his hand on his son's shoulder. Étienne smiled briefly. "After the English surrendered and opened the gates," he continued, "the French and Indians broke into the barrels of rum that were stored inside the walls and started to plunder the fort. The English were prisoners. They couldn't escape. They tried." Étienne shuddered. "They were cut down by the drunks. Scalped. Blood and bodies everywhere. I can't get it out of my head."

Jacques forced down the nausea that threatened to overwhelm him. "The French?" he whispered.

"Yes, the French! There was no control, no authority… they didn't care."

Étienne leaned back, fighting the pain and the memories that rushed in on him. "It was all so senseless," he muttered.

"But we didn't start the war," Jacques protested. "The English…"

"Oh, Jacques." Étienne whispered. He looked at his brother and Jacques could see the despair in his eyes. He closed his mouth.

For a moment everyone was silent. Henri seemed to shrink, hiding his head in his hands. Anne dropped the needle she was holding and came to stand behind her husband, stroking his hair. Michel sat motionless on the stool, the carving resting on his knee. Maman sighed.

Finally Papa spoke. "It doesn't matter who started it this time," he said. "The English and the French have been fighting off and on for generations. It's one of the reasons my great-grandfather went to L'Acadie. All he wanted to do was to farm in peace."

Henri raised his head and took Anne's hands in his. "That's all we wanted too. To live in Grand-Pré with our family and neighbours, to raise our children…"

Jacques' chest ached. "I know," he whispered, "but…

our language, our religion…We don't belong here. We're not English, we are French."

"Non," Papa said. "We are Acadian. The French in Québec and Louisbourg are merchants and soldiers. We speak the same language, yes, but that is all we have in common. They did not come to L'Acadie to settle, not really. And they never cared about us."

Suddenly, Jacques felt a deep weariness flood through his body, as though his very bones were melting. For the first time, the anger and certainty he had felt since Étienne had left their home in Grand-Pré was gone, replaced by sadness and exhaustion. While Papa and Henri lifted Étienne onto his makeshift bed beside the table and Maman cleared away the quilt she and Anne had been working on, he sat and stared into the fire. Then he got up and followed Michel up the ladder to the loft.

FIFTEEN

The Barn Raising

Jacques braced his weight on his back foot, straining to hold the log in front of him steady as Henri and Mr. Thompson fitted it into the slot cut into the wooden upright. Papa and one of the neighbourhood men gripped the other end. The log slipped into the groove, and Jacques dropped his arms with a groan. His back and shoulders ached, and sweat ran into his eyes, making them burn. He rubbed the back of his hand across his forehead, watching as the men struggled to fit the other end into the framework of the new barn. Jacques took a step back, looking up at the structure which had slowly taken shape since early that morning, when men from farms all over Weymouth had come to help Mr. Thompson replace the barn that had burned earlier in the fall.

"A good effort today." Étienne came to stand beside his brother. In the month since he rode into the yard and almost fell from his horse, Étienne had grown stronger. There was colour in his face and arms from working outside, although his chores, like Michel's, involved caring for the animals and cutting firewood in preparation for the coming winter. The slash on his arm was still red against his browned skin, but it had healed cleanly and he could move the arm, though stiffly.

"Oui," Jacques agreed. "We should be able to finish tomorrow." He stretched his arms over his head. "But now I'm exhausted."

"The women have been cooking all day," Étienne said. "Let's get something to eat."

"Un moment." Jacques walked over to the rain barrel at the corner of the house and splashed water on his face and over his head. He shivered as the icy water dripped down his bare back. He grabbed his shirt from the pile on the ground, shook it, and pulled it on. Brushing the hair out of his face, he looked around.

The sun was sinking behind the pasture fence, giving way to the dull twilight of autumn. Like Jacques, most of the men were picking up their tools, easing the aches in their backs, and pulling on the clothes they'd stripped off in the afternoon heat. Mr. Thompson, Henri and Papa stood together beside the barn, gesturing as they planned the next step in the building. The women and older girls piled steaming dishes on crudely-built tables outside the door of the main house, while Marguerite and the other children chased each other around and across the bright quilts laid out on the carpet of fallen leaves.

"Do you remember Martin Doucette's barn-raising?" Étienne pushed him out of the way and stuck his arms in the rain barrel. "What a day that was! The sun shining, and the colours blazing! Everyone singing…"

"And petite Marie smiling and fluttering her eyes at you!" Jacques said.

Étienne splashed cold water at him. Jacques laughed.

"It was just before..." Étienne looked down, wiping his hands on his trousers. "We didn't know..."

Jacques swallowed. "The English burnt it down," he said harshly.

Étienne nodded, and they stared at their feet, each lost in his own thoughts.

"Here." The girl's voice made Jacques jump. He looked up to see Elizabeth with two mugs. "You looked hot. I brought you some cider."

Jacques took one of the cups. "Merci."

"De rien!" Elizabeth grinned at Jacques' look of surprise. "Your maman has been teaching me a few words of French," she said. She placed the other mug in Étienne's outstretched hand. "Le souper sera bientôt prêt," she said carefully. She turned and walked away.

Jacques stared after her in amazement. Étienne chuckled and took a drink. Jacques turned on him, suddenly furious. "How can you laugh," he demanded. "The English have stolen everything! Are they stealing our language now?"

Étienne scowled. "Assez!" he said impatiently. "She's just trying to be friendly. When are you going to admit it? The people here are not like the English soldiers."

"Winslow was from New England," Jacques said.

"Oui," Étienne replied. "But he was a soldier. He had to follow orders. Just as I did." A slight shudder ran through him, and he took a gulp of cider.

Jacques studied him. Since he had told his story of the battle of Oswego, Étienne had stubbornly refused to talk more about it. When Jacques tried to question him, Étienne merely repeated, "Papa avait raison."

"How can you forgive them?" he asked softly.

Étienne sighed. Holding his cider in one hand, he put his other hand on Jacques' elbow and guided him away from the crowd beginning to surround the tables. They walked without talking towards the pasture where the horses were quietly cropping grass. The stallion lifted its head to stare at the boys as they leaned against the wooden fence.

"It's the only choice we have," Étienne said at last. "You're right. The English took everything—our homes, our land, everything. And they gave it away to their allies." His hands gripped the railing. "We can't ever get it back. Even if we fight for a thousand years…" He looked at Jacques, and his face was wet with tears. "Do you think I don't miss it too? Don't you know I would give anything…?"

Jacques put his arm around his brother's shoulders. "Then why forgive?" he whispered.

Étienne spun away from him. "Because, if we don't, they win!" he shouted. "Don't you understand?" He threw his mug. The cider splashed as it smashed against the trunk of a nearby tree. His hands clenched into fists, as his shoulders shook with his sobs.

Jacques sank onto the ground and covered his face with his hands. "Non," he said. "I don't understand."

For a long time, neither boy spoke. A light breeze carried the sound of voices and laughter along with the smell of roasted meat. Finally, Étienne slid down to sit beside his brother.

"Regardes," he said. He lifted Jacques chin with one hand and pointed towards the house.

Jacques looked. He saw Anne and Elizabeth stretched out on one of the brightly coloured quilts, Marguerite jumping up and down between them as they sang and clapped their hands. Although he couldn't make out the words, Jacques recognized it as a song Maman had taught him when he was young. Papa, deep in conversation with Mr. Thompson and Michel, turned to grin at them. Maman, standing beside one of the tables, handed a plate of food to Henri and a couple of the neighbourhood men, then peered around the yard.

"She's looking for us," Étienne said, and waved. Maman beckoned for them to come.

Étienne stood up. "Now do you understand?" he asked. He walked towards the others.

Jacques watched as Étienne snatched Marguerite from the blanket and spun her around. The little girl's laughter filled the yard. For a moment, the tightness in Jacques' chest eased and he smiled. He heard Papa's words echoing inside his head, the words he had spoken so long ago. "There's only one way we can win," Papa had said. "By fighting with our ploughs and our families. Not with guns."

Peut-être, he thought as he got to his feet, just maybe, Papa was right.

French words, phrases and place names

French	English
À bientôt, mon frère	See you later, my brother
Arrête	Stop
Assez	Enough
Asseyez-vous	Sit down
Beaubassin	An Acadian village in present-day Nova Scotia, near New Brunswick
Beauséjour	A French fort, located near present-day Moncton, New Brunswick
Bien	Good
Bienvenue	Welcome
Bravo	Well done, congratulations
C'est vrai	That's right/true
Ce serait bien	That would be good
Chignecto	The area around Beaubassin
Contente	Happy, glad
De rien	No problem
Demain	Tomorrow
Dieu merci	Thank God
Et meilleure nourriture	And better food
Excusez-moi	Excuse me
Grand-Pré	An Acadian village on the Minas Basin, in present-day Nova Scotia
Heureusement	Fortunately
Jamais	Never
Je sais	I know
L'Acadie	Acadia French colony in present-day Nova Scotia
L'Acadie toujours	Acadia forever
Laisse la tranquille	Leave her alone
Lentement	Slowly
Le souper sera bientôt prêt	Supper will be ready soon
Louisbourg	A French fortress located on Cape Breton Island

Ma petite/mon petit .... My little one
Maintenant .... Now
Mais .... But
Mais peut-etre demain .... But maybe tomorrow
Maman .... Mother, mommy
Marchand .... Merchant
Maudit .... Cursed
Merci .... Thank you
Merde .... A French swear word
Mon Dieu .... My God
Mon frère .... My brother
Non .... No
Ou souper .... Or supper
Oui .... Yes
Papa avait raison .... Papa is right
Parlez-vous .... Do you speak
Pas encore .... Not yet
Pas ici .... Not here
Peut-être pas .... Maybe not
Pisiquid .... Fort Edward, located near
                                          present-day Windsor, Nova Scotia
Port Royal .... French name for present-day
                                          Annapolis Royal, Nova Scotia
Qu'est-ce que tu fais ici? .... What are you doing here?
Quelle différence ça fait? .... What difference does it make?
Regardes .... Look
Reste ici .... Stay here
Sœurs .... Sisters
Tatamagouche .... An Acadian village located close
                                          to present-day Truro, Nova Scotia
Très facile .... Very easy
Tric-trac .... A game similar to backgammon
Tu parles anglais? .... You speak English?
Un garçon cabine .... Cabin boy
Un peu .... A little

Acknowledgements

Many people contributed to the shaping and growth of this book. I would like to thank the Centre d'études acadiennes at the Université de Moncton, the Fédération Acadienne de La Nouvelle-Écosse, the Boston Public Library, and Massachusetts Archives for their assistance with my research. I would like to thank my husband for accompanying me to Boston to do that research, and all my family and friends who read the manuscript and gave me suggestions and encouragement. I would like to thank my publishers, for seeing the potential in my novel and helping me to revise, edit and produce the best possible version. And finally, I want to thank my readers—I hope you love my story as much as I do!

Anne C. Kelly

Anne C. Kelly is the English Language Learning Coordinator at the Bedford Library and also works with Learn English Nova Scotia, completing English language assessments. She previously worked for over twenty years providing English-as-an-additional-language (EAL) support to newcomers to Canada. She is married with four grown children, has been writing since Grade Four, and is passionate about books and Canadian history.